THAT TIME I LOVED YOU

THAT TIME I LOVED YOU

Stories

CARRIANNE LEUNG

LIVERIGHT PUBLISHING CORPORATION

A DIVISION OF W. W. NORTON & COMPANY

Independent Publishers Since 1923

NEW YORK   LONDON

For information about permission to reproduce selections from this book,
write to Permissions, Liveright Publishing Corporation,
a division of W. W. Norton & Company, Inc.,
500 Fifth Avenue, New York, NY 10110

For information about special discounts for bulk purchases, please contact
W. W. Norton Special Sales at specialsales@wwnorton.com or 800-233-4830

Manufacturing by Sheridan

ISBN 978-1-63149-552-6

Liveright Publishing Corporation
500 Fifth Avenue, New York, N.Y. 10110
www.wwnorton.com

W. W. Norton & Company Ltd.
15 Carlisle Street, London W1D 3BS

1 2 3 4 5 6 7 8 9 0

To Fenn Archdekin-Leung
I'll always tell you stories

Contents

Grass

1979: This was the year the parents in my neighbourhood began killing themselves. I was eleven years old and in Grade 6. Elsewhere in the world, big things were happening. McDonald's introduced the Happy Meal, Ayatollah Khomeini returned to Iran and Michael Jackson released his album *Off the Wall*. But none of that was as significant to me as the suicides.

It started with Mr. Finley, Carolyn Finley's dad. It was a Saturday afternoon in freezing February. My best friend, Josie, and I were sitting on her bed, playing Barry Manilow's "Copacabana" over and over again on her cassette player and writing down the lyrics. I was the recorder while Josie pressed play, rewind, and play again a hundred times, repeating the lines over to me until the ribbon finally snapped and we had to repair it with Scotch tape.

"Did you get that, June? Did you get that?" she kept asking me as I nodded and wrote furiously on lined paper.

We kept all the transcribed lyrics in a special pink binder marked "SONGS" in my balloon lettering.

I didn't like the song as much as she did and wanted to switch to "Le Freak" to practise our new dance moves, but Josie was determined to unravel the mystery of Lola at the Copa.

Josie's brother, Tim, came in the front door, slammed it hard and thumped up the stairs, shouting, "Josie! June! Mr. Finley's dead. He's dead! He's fucking dead!"

At first, I thought Tim was angry at Mr. Finley. We often were mad at him because he was our softball coach and mean. Then I realized by the sound of Tim's voice that he was serious, that Mr. Finley was dead dead.

Tim burst into Josie's room to tell us the grisly details. Mr. Finley had offed himself with one of the hunting rifles he kept in a display case in his basement, beside his collection of taxidermied animal heads. His daughter, Carolyn, was in my class. The one time I had a sleepover at her house, we'd slept in the basement. Dead deer and owl and bear heads had cast eerie shadows on the walls. She'd snuggled into her Benji sleeping bag and drifted off while I was as rigid as the snarling heads above me and didn't dare close my eyes, fearing that even in their current state they'd go for my jugular. Josie and I had never been invited to a white family's house before, which is why I had said yes, and after I told Josie all about the horror show, we assumed all white people decorated their homes with dead animal parts. No thank you very much.

Mr. Finley was the first person in the neighbourhood to kill himself. It gave me the chills. Not long after that, Georgie Da Silva's mother, on a warm June night, shuffled out to their double garage and drank a jar of Javex bleach. At 8:30 a.m., Georgie went looking for her when he didn't see her in the kitchen. He found her body sprawled on the oil-stained floor, a stream of white sudsy liquid pouring from her nose and mouth, her eyes looking right at him. That's what all the kids on the street said. We all began to worry: This was my and most of my friends' first experience of death. It was kind of exciting at first, but then it got scary. Would there be another one? And another after that?

The suicides all happened on what we called the "sister streets." Our neighbourhood was made up of three streets that ran parallel to one another and were joined by a bigger street running perpendicular. Winifred, Maud and Clara Streets all met on Samuel Avenue. I imagined Winifred, Maud and Clara were sisters from olden times, like in *Little Women*, my favourite book. Maybe Samuel was their brother, who'd gone off to war. The three sister streets were almost carbon copies of each other, with the same houses—three two-storeys and a bungalow repeated as a pattern—mostly the same cars in the driveways—Fords, Hondas and an occasional Volkswagen—and some form of fruit tree. On my street, Winifred, were crabapples, Maud had cherries and Clara Street's trees bore plums so sour no one could eat them. These trees were bred to be miniature, so we could never get high enough for

3

a view from their twiggy branches or eat any of the gnatty fruit that fell down and rotted quietly in the grass.

The three sisters streets and their brother, Samuel Avenue, contained my world, all of our homeland operations. All my friends lived here, my school was down the street on Samuel and in the other direction was the way to the plaza with Mac's Milk, Hunter's Pizza and Bamboo Garden, which sold takeout Chinese food that my parents said was not real Chinese food. On the other side of the plaza was the "old part" of the neighbourhood, where people had been living longer.

That summer, as they watered their front lawns, the adults leaned across their fences and spoke in hushed voices, flooding their grass with their now forgotten hoses. Us kids gathered in the street with our road hockey gear and baseballs to share whatever intel we'd acquired and trade in gory details. Mr. Finley's brain was supposedly splattered in a million bits across his basement. My friend Darren said you couldn't clean brain completely out—that stuff sticks. Darren knew a lot about brains because he was into comic books and his mother was a nurse, so we took whatever he said as fact. As for Mrs. Da Silva, everybody knew she wasn't right in the head. We often saw her walking around in her housecoat talking and laughing to herself.

Nothing like this had ever happened in our quiet suburban neighbourhood before. No one had even died before Mr. Finley. In downtown Toronto, where the dangerous people lived, at least according to my dad, it probably happened all the time. Dad said downtown was no place for kids because it was dirty and full of fast cars and shady characters, while out here in the suburbs, we were free to play on the street, leave our front doors unlocked and generally not worry about such things. Granted, there was a neighbourhood thief sneaking around, but only small, mostly worthless things were taken—forgotten gardening gloves on the lawn, chipped coffee mugs left on the porch, a rusty screwdriver in a garage. People assumed it was some weird kid's idea of fun. I had my own opinion on who it was, and it was no kid. But no one listened to me anyway.

My street, like the rest of the subdivision, was brand new. Most of the neighbours had moved in four years ago, right after the houses were finished. My parents loved the neat grid of black road, the bright white stripes to differentiate the lanes, the chain-linked fences that divided our properties but gave us views into the neighbours' yards, the young, weeping trees lining our streets. They said you couldn't get "all this" in Hong Kong, where everybody was crammed on top of each other in tiny apartments, and they would sweep their arms to include whatever "all this" referred to, like showcase girls on *The Price Is Right*. They were always saying, "June, you don't know how lucky you are that you were born here and not there." Mom and Dad had come to this country on student visas fifteen years ago, but the way they told it, it was like they were fresh off the boat. But I suppose they had lived in the city for those years in crammed apartments, and moving out here to the suburbs, Mom and Dad finally got some land. Even though it was only a square lawn and a rectangular backyard, this was a big deal. Land was land.

Between the road tar and the pine boards and the wall-to-wall carpeting, the whole place smelled like a new toy just unwrapped. The kids liked to guess what the area had been before they bulldozed it and put up our houses: Farmland, cemetery, someone else's neighbourhood? But that was for sport. It was brand spanking new and made you feel like anything was possible.

As soon as the houses were built, we all moved in. My parents and I moved from our two-bedroom apartment downtown to our four-bedroom spread of a house in Scarborough. It was only a thirty-minute drive between the two places by highway, but my parents were convinced that the air was even cleaner in the new neighbourhood. At first, it had felt like Disneyland. Since it was the beginning of summer, the heat got us outside, and everybody got to know each other and planned things like fireworks and barbecues on the long weekends. Everybody was invited at first, but then it seemed like people decided who their friends were, and the invitations that used to be shoved in all the mailboxes stopped coming. It was the same for us kids. We met, sized each other up and broke into groups. Things settled into routines.

The suicides changed that. I heard a neighbour say, "But it had all been going so well!" I didn't know if it was my ears, but he sounded angry, like he'd been let down, as if the local team lost a hockey game even though the captain promised they were going to smash it.

Even though kids from other neighbourhoods went to my school, my very best friends all happened to live on the sister streets. They included the other Chinese families—the Wongs, the Chows, the Changs. Josie was a Chow. My dad said we were Chinese from Hong Kong, not like the Toishan Chinese downtown, who had been here longer and were from villages back in China.

It wasn't because we were Chinese that we were friends. It just happened that way. There were others who hung out with us, like Nav, who was Indian but "India Indian" and not "Native Indian," as he would have to explain many times, and Darren, who was Jamaican or Black depending on who was talking. There were also a lot of white kids, but they didn't play in the streets in packs like we did and tended to go to each other's houses with tote bags full of Barbies and G.I. Joes. There were some Italian and Portuguese kids and they played in groups. They also mostly kept to themselves and we didn't play with them very often. We stayed on Winifred while they played on Maud. This arrangement quickly became the way it was. We tried a shared game of volleyball once, stringing a net on one of our sloped driveways. One side was always screaming foul for having to play against gravity, which almost led to the first-ever gang rumble on our street.

Regardless of which group we belonged to—Chinese, white or otherwise—by the second suicide, it felt like we were waiting for something else catastrophic to happen. We were nervous enough to pool our information across the group divides. Like the Hardy Boys and Nancy Drew, we started watching our parents carefully, taking note of unusual things. On a Thursday in June, after the school year ended, Cindy Taylor from down at the end of Winifred told us that her father, who put a lot of stock into being well groomed, went to work with a wrinkled white shirt beneath his blue blazer and forgot to shave. Did this mean something? We patted her back, unable to say for sure. Stephanie Papadakis said her mother forgot to put garlic in their moussaka one night, and she *never* forgot to put garlic in the moussaka. It was easy to jump to conclusions, assume these signs were the beginning of the end. I was a good watcher anyway and observed everything just in case I needed the information for later, but that summer, I made sure to pay extra attention to everything.

My parents were their regular selves. They still worked their same long hours at their office jobs, so I could only watch them before bed and on weekends, and I couldn't detect a thing. My dad still didn't talk to me much, same as always, shooing me away while he read the paper or watched the news. My mother told me to stop staring at her because I was making her nervous. She was busy getting papers filled out and seeing the lawyer about sponsoring Poh Poh, my grandmother from Hong Kong, to come live with us. When I finally asked her about the deaths, my mother said, "There's more than meets the eye." She liked English sayings. She said they were great conversation starters, and she used them a lot in the staff lunchroom at the office where she worked as a keypunch operator. I knew the suicides got to my parents. The creased lines on their foreheads and the pursed lips that lingered long after my questions made my stomach ache.

Because my parents didn't get home until close to six p.m., I spent my main observation time with an eye on Liz, Josie's sixteen-year-old sister, who looked after me while she was parked on the couch watching soap operas or reading Harlequin romances. I'd never met anyone so boring. I thought I might be the one who died from watching her.

After Mr. Finley joined the spirits of the dead animal heads in his basement, Carolyn got sent to her grandparents' place in the country. We waved goodbye as her grandfather's wood-panelled Ford station wagon pulled out of her driveway and wound down our long street. We chased it until it turned left onto Samuel, and kept waving long after the car had disappeared. I thought I saw Carolyn crying as she drove away. For a long while, it seemed like their house was empty, even though we knew her mother was still there. A month went by, and it was put up for sale. We wondered if the brains were finally cleaned up or whether someone had painted over them.

Georgie Da Silva took to sitting on a lawn chair in his

garage with the doors wide open, and everyone who passed by could see him sitting right by the spot where his mom died. For the first few days, his Italian and Portuguese gang gathered around him, gently punching him in the arm and sitting on the ground at his feet, listening to the radio and smoking quietly. Some brought flowers and laid them on the driveway. But when that ended, it was just Georgie, staring at some spot on the ground for hours each day while we played Frisbee football up the road.

It barely rained that summer, and in the sweet, warm air, we made the hours worth it. We met in the morning, dew still on the grass, to play baseball, ball hockey and that game that was a cross between tag and hide and seek, stopping only for lemonade at someone's house and baloney sandwiches for lunch, staying out until the first street lamp flickered on. Sometimes we would forget all about the suicides because our games would be so fun, but then a kid would come running up the street with some new observation to report, and we remembered. It was too difficult to play hard and be scared at the same time.

It was around the time of Mrs. Da Silva's suicide that my dad developed a weird friendship with the white boy Larry Lems, the class bully who lived on Maud. Larry had come to our door one day and asked my dad if he could mow the lawn for him or do some odd jobs. When I heard his voice, I ran upstairs to my room like a scared rabbit. At school, everyone knew to keep their distance. Larry hated all the kids not just in our class but in all of Grade 6. He called us by a variety of names depending on what bothered him about us: Sean was Fatso, Cindy was Fucking Idiot, Damian was Retard, Darren was Nigger, Nav was Faggot, Sena was Motor Mouth, Maria was Wop, my best friend, Josie, was Chink #1, and, because Larry didn't have much of an imagination or vocabulary, I got Chink #2. He stole our lunches, pushed us over even if we weren't in his way, and challenged all the boys to fights after school, which he nearly always won except that one time Darren got in a good shot and gave him a bloody nose. Darren confided in me after that he had pretended he was the Thing from the Fantastic Four and this did the trick to give him the extra power to clobber Larry. And besides, Darren said, no one called him a nigger and got away with it. That made him such a hero that for weeks afterward, we gifted him with all the choice items from our lunches, the Peek Freans jam-filled cookies, packs of Bubblicious gum, mini bags of Humpty Dumpty chips. That was how much we hated Larry Lems.

So when he showed up at our house, I was naturally horrified when I heard my dad say "Sure" and offer Larry some jobs to do around our house. He even let Larry use his prized 1974 twenty-one-inch model 7263 Lawn Boy with the two-stroke engine, which he would never let me or my mom even touch because he claimed we would cut ourselves for sure since women couldn't understand the true power of the machine. It was no secret that the Lawn Boy was my father's real baby. He had purchased it from Sears the first summer we were in the house. He was pretty lazy about mowing the lawn, but for whatever reason, he loved his mower. He kept the engine well oiled and the blades as sharp as Ginsu knives. He let Larry use the Lawn Boy to cut the grass and also had him weed the flower beds for three dollars. When I heard that arrangement, I almost passed out. Three dollars? He didn't deserve three cents.

Our backyard had always been a jungle of neglect. Since my parents had day jobs, I was like the latch-key kids the TV news talked about, and there wasn't much free time or interest on anybody's part in tending to the yard. But by late afternoon of that first day Larry worked for us, the yard looked good. The grass was neat, free of the choking dandelions and clover. It was as if the whole backyard heaved a sigh of relief. When my dad went out to talk to Larry, I braced myself for the name-calling. My dad had a lot of nervous ticks; his left eye twitched, and his arms would sporadically shoot into the air while he talked, so he'd elbow himself in the ribs several times during a conversation. All this plus the fact that my dad was a chink added up to choice meat for Larry Lems. But it never came. I peered down at them from my bedroom window. With his arms akimbo, my dad checked Larry's work, nodding with approval. Larry, swigging the can of Pepsi my dad had given him, was hon-est-to-God smiling. It occurred to me that I had never seen him smile before.

From that day on, Larry came over every week. I still scrambled away at the first sign of him and tore out to the street to be with my friends. It would take a whole lot more than him cracking a smile for me to believe he had changed. My dad found him odd jobs to do and gave him a dollar or two each time. One Saturday, he even showed Larry how to take the Lawn Boy apart and put it back together again, explaining the function of each part. I watched how Larry paid close attention as my dad squirted oil on the bolts and gently removed the blades. He then taught Larry how to hold the blades at the exact angle they needed to be for the grinder to scrape at the edge. He let Larry hold the blades to try to sharpen them himself. Larry looked like he was in heaven. He looked like a kid and not some axe murderer. My father also seemed to enjoy his time with Larry, giving him his complete attention. I figured it was because Larry was a boy.

They worked in the driveway, unaware that I was watch-ing from a safe distance in the street. Darren came by and shot me a big-eyed look after seeing Larry and my dad. I shrugged, embarrassed that my own father was working with the enemy. But I didn't have an answer.

I wouldn't have minded as much if my dad became friends with someone normal. But Larry, the human freak of nature? He hit a teacher once with closed fists, I told my dad. He tripped a mom in the schoolyard while she was carrying her baby. But my dad didn't listen. He told me that people needed chances to show who they really were. I screamed and cried, slammed doors—to no avail. My mother shrugged and said, "Those who live in glass houses shouldn't cast stones," which made less and less sense the more I thought about it.

One day, my dad crossed the line. I was coming down the stairs and saw Larry sitting in our kitchen, at the table where we ate, bent over a birdhouse that my dad had bought but never got around to putting together. My dad stood behind him reading the instructions aloud, with a hand on Larry's shoulder. That did it. This was my house and I'd had enough of feeling like a prisoner in my room every time Larry showed up, so I pretended I wanted a glass of water and sauntered in. Larry lifted his head and said, "Hi, June." Not "Hey, Chink #2. What chinky thing are you doing today?" Just like that, like a normal human being. I was surprised that he even knew my name. My dad gave me a told-you-so kind of grin. I had no ammunition if the boy was going to act normal on me.

Fortunately, Larry only came to work at our house on the weekends. Mr. Lems was a drunk, and sometimes in the mornings as we were going to school, we'd catch a glimpse of him with his skinny white pecs and flabby, little, pasty ball of a stomach reflecting the sun, muttering about the damned squirrels on the roof waking him up. Once, he spent an entire morning shooting at them with a BB gun. No one knew anything about Larry's mother, but I overheard the women on the block saying that they didn't blame her for leaving *that*. They only blamed her for leaving Larry too.

Then came the Saturday when my dad's lawn mower went missing. It didn't seem like the doing of the neighbourhood thief. My mom lost a teacup once, but a lawn mower? Now, that was different, and I couldn't help the satisfied smile on my face when I told my dad I knew where he'd find it. He looked sad, like he knew it was true but didn't want to believe that Larry would take it. A few afternoons later, he finally shuffled over to Larry's. When he returned, rolling the Lawn Boy up the driveway, it was after dark. My mother and I watched him from the front door. He barely looked at us when he pushed through, went to the living room and plunked down into his recliner. My mother sighed and said, "The apple doesn't fall far from the tree." I wanted to say something smart, like the crabapples on his street were small and wormy and sour like lemons, which would make sense given the situation, but I held my tongue.

In the dim light of his armchair lamp, my dad looked tired. He rubbed his eyes with the backs of his hands. "That Mr. Lems is a rough, rough man," he began. Ma and I stood patiently beside him like soldiers. He said that Larry denied everything until his father dragged him to the garage by his hair and found the lawn mower hidden behind some lumber. My dad could only watch as Mr. Lems called Larry all kinds of names that children shouldn't ever hear. Then Mr. Lems made like he would take Larry outside to give him a whupping. My dad tried to smooth things out, but Mr. Lems wouldn't hear of anything less than a beating and even invited my dad to give Larry a whack. My dad suggested instead that as punishment Larry could come over and work for him for free. He said Larry's dad reeked of Scotch and it took a long time to convince him to calm down. The most horrible part was when Mr. Lems relaxed and even joked with him and made light of the whole thing. Larry was silent and stayed in the corner of the room. When my dad left, he said he didn't know how to feel. Empty beer bottles and fast-food wrappers covered every counter and overflowed in the garbage can. "Poor kid," he kept repeating. "Poor kid."

The next week, Larry did come over. It was a Sunday afternoon, and my dad and I were busy scaling some large-mouth bass we'd caught up in Lindsay at our favourite fishing hole under a highway bridge. We had squatted on rocks for hours in the dark and early dawn while my mom poured tea for us from a Thermos. We had a good catch that day. The silvery bits were flying in the air all around the sink like rain. My mom was getting out the steamer so she could cook them with ginger and green onions, when we heard some sounds coming from the garage. My dad ran through the back door to see what it was. He found Larry cutting the cord of the Lawn Boy with a pair of garden shears.

Larry startled when he saw my dad and backed up. He was crying, tears streaming down his face. "Stay away from me, you fucking chink!" he screamed. My dad froze. "Stay out of my life, or I swear I'm going to kill you and your whole chink family." He turned and ran out of the garage and down the street, his knapsack bouncing around his back. My dad held the two parts of the cord in his hands and gazed down the road. He looked back at the Lawn Boy, frowned and turned it upside down. The blades were gone. I watched the whole scene from the shadows behind the garage door. It made me feel like bawling, but I didn't.

Five days later, Jimmy Farley, who was Larry's next-door neighbour, told us how his dad had found Mr. Lems stone-cold dead. Mr. Farley had noticed a bad smell like rotten eggs coming from the Lemses' house and thought he should check up on them. The door was unlocked when Mr. Farley knocked, so he went in. The place stank from old garbage and the pungent sweet-sour smell of a dumped-out whisky bottle. Mr. Lems was lying on the couch, and the TV was on. He looked like he could have been sleeping, but Jimmy told us that his dad said his body was bloated. Darren confirmed this, since his mother was on nursing duty at the hospital where Mr. Lems was brought. Darren's mother had explained to him that dead bodies do that because gases get released and sometimes trapped. We imagined that bodies might even explode from all the gases.

The big question that us kids had was *Was this another suicide?* It didn't seem like it was. Mr. Lems lay down and died. Darren's mother had told him that the doctors called it a "death from natural causes." But when Darren prodded her some more, his mother said that sometimes killing yourself is slow and takes time. That maybe you aren't even aware you are doing it, but you're doing it anyway.

More things that made no sense, but what she said stayed with me.

When Mr. Lems's body was discovered, Larry was nowhere to be found. Mr. Farley looked for him in the house, with his handkerchief held over his nose, but the boy was gone. Later, Larry's mother surfaced to pack up the house and told the neighbours that her son had been with her for the past week and hadn't been anywhere near the body.

And that was it. The next day, my dad packed up the Lawn Boy and drove it to the dump. When he came back, he sat out in the backyard staring into space for a long, long time. My mother and I pulled up lawn chairs and sat beside him. I wanted to say something, but I didn't know what would make him feel better. Besides, my dad never looked at me; his eyes remained on that empty space while I stared at his thin lips.

Dusk came and the sweet scent of the grass enveloped us. The white roses Larry had cleared from the weeds in the back corner by the fence gleamed, and crickets began to chirp. Off in the distance, some people were having a barbecue. I could smell the scent of charred meat and hear murmurs and laughter. I looked across the fences to the expanse of green that was our neighbourhood. It looked like it went on forever, as if it were the whole world and nothing else existed. My mother combed her fingers through my hair, something she never did, and said softly, "As beautiful as the day is long."

Flowers

On that day, the last day, the primroses were especially pretty. Their red petals opened to kiss the summer sun. Mrs. Da Silva's first thought upon waking that morning was to water them. She had tossed and turned all night in a restless sleep and woke up already tired. There had been no rain for days. In her faded cotton house dress, she pulled the garden hose from its long coil attached to the concrete wall of the house. She liked the ease of the garden hose, its coil, its simple tap, its reach. Everything was easy here, compared with Portugal. You had a house with a tap attached to the side wall. You turned it on and water came from the hose. After twenty years in this country, Mrs. D was still amazed. Spraying the water across the patch of grass and on the petals of the primroses was among her favourite things. Each blade of grass and small flower shook and shivered under the mist raining down. When she turned, the flowers whispered two words in Portuguese behind her back that sounded like a sigh: *The letter*.

Her finger released the lever of the nozzle on her hose. She stood silently in the glistening grass, her toes getting wet through her slippers. She waited to hear more, but the flowers went silent. Mrs. D wondered how the flowers knew about the letter, but then she remembered that they knew everything about her, as if there were an invisible thread that ran between them. The letter had arrived two days earlier, and she had read it, memorized its contents, but the news didn't seem real, more like a ghostly whisper from far away. Only when the flowers uttered the words in their familiar accent, as if they too had come from her fishing village in São Miguel, did the letter feel true. There were facts in the letter. The flowers confirmed it. Her *mãe*, her beautiful mother, was dead.

Mrs. D dropped the hose, the water still running, and walked into her garage. The cool darkness comforted her body. She felt sweat gathering in her armpits. Away from the sun, where everything sparkled and blinded, the darkness was a relief. She eased her body down on a lawn chair, filling it. Her body, so angular and lean when she was young, was now soft and padded. She spent a lot of time here in the garage, sometimes with the doors wide open, sitting at its threshold, so she could look at her garden and talk to the flowers. It was perfect, this spot, neither outside nor in. She liked to have a roof over her head. Also, she liked to be close to the laundry. Mrs. D had a washer and a big tumbling machine that dried clothes. Whirlpool. They were very good and efficient. Still, after she removed the damp clothes from the washer, she preferred to hang them. It's how her mother did it, and how she was taught to do it back home. They did it together, high up in the hills with the wind whipping their skirts, the tall grass swaying, and beyond, the sea. Where the sweet scent of ginger lilies that grew along the coast floated up to them. These were her happiest memories with her mother. Her hands rhythmically pinned the damp clothes, releasing them to the gales. She did her part, so the sun and breeze could do theirs. Afterward, she would stand beside the fluttering linen and spread her arms out, legs wide, and face the sun, the clouds, the sea, the wind and grass. She would close her eyes and become part of the world.

Even here in this new country, in this quiet neighbourhood away from the big city, where the houses were protected from the elements and things were easy, even during the wintertime, Mrs. D wanted to hang the clothes. She asked for a clothesline to be mounted in the garage. Her husband said she was crazy. He wouldn't do such a fucking thing when he had bought her a washer and dryer, he'd said, and slapped her for her foolishness. Later, she asked her child, Georgie, to do it. Georgie loved her, and so he did. He was too short to reach up to the crossbeams, but he pulled out his father's ladder and hammered the nails and fastened the line. Georgie did this even though he knew his father would hit him when he found out. And sure enough,

Georgie's father did hit him, but for whatever reason, the line was left up.

Sometimes in the coldest months, when Mrs. D would come out to the garage, the clothes would be frozen. Like cardboard dolls, stiff on the line. This made her laugh. She had a bark of laughter like a small dog sounding short and urgent warnings to others. There were years when nothing had made her laugh, and she had walked like a shadow through her days. When she first arrived in this country, she had been afraid of everything. At first, she told Mr. D about her fear. "Sometimes the doorbell rings when you are away. I am afraid of answering the door." He told her to shut up. "I am afraid of going to the store by myself. They say things to me I don't understand." He told her to get off her ass and buy some food. "I am afraid to go out in winter. It's so cold. I am afraid I may freeze like they do in the Tom and Jerry cartoon and die." He slapped her with an open palm.

But one day, all her clothespins went missing. She didn't know where they went or who could have taken them, but she became even more afraid. She held the fear inside her body like a shiver. Mrs. D paid special attention to what Mr. D expected—she bought the food, answered the door, went out in the cold, opened her legs—but always with the shiver inside her. Sometimes she shivered so hard, she thought her body might crack open and shatter, but she never spoke of it.

Then, like a miracle, one spring day, the flowers started to talk. At first, she was confused by the murmuring, but then she listened hard. They were talking to her! They were funny, sometimes naughty or mean, but they talked. Flowers talking—it was so absurd—and the idea of it caused her to laugh so hard her stomach ached. They asked her in unison, "Who are you? Who am I?"

On this day, sitting in her garage, on the edge of the lovely morning, she decided that today would be the final day. On this day, she would go home, to her real home, away from this hose, away from this house in the middle of the block. The other day, Georgie showed her his first paycheque from working part-time with his father on the construction site. Mr. D had clapped his hand across Georgie's back and offered a rare smile. Georgie, her boy, was a man now. And her mother was dead. The flowers had been telling her for a long time to go, but now she understood. They were right. She had been waiting for some release from the heaviness that had been building in her body. This weight had pinned her to this life, where nothing seemed to make sense no matter how hard she tried. Only Georgie made sense, and now, he didn't need her anymore. She could fly away if she wanted. Her mother was leading the way. The signs were there.

She swung open the garage doors and picked up the hose. She turned and sprayed the driveway and the sidewalk in front of their house. This last time, she wanted to do an extra-good job making everything clean. The red flowers beside the walkway leading to her front door turned their faces up at her again to say, "The letter." Mrs. D nodded to show that she had heard.

They had a right to be intrusive; they'd lived there almost as long as she had. Mr. D planted them when they first moved into the house. They were expensive, she remembered him saying, but they would come back every season. They came back like noisy relatives each year.

She took care of them, but it was Mr. D whom they loved. They preened and giggled like lovestruck girls when he walked by. They loved Georgie too, whistling and shouting, "How handsome!" when he was near. With Mrs. D, they weren't so kind, and sometimes she had to bend down close to catch their discreet whispers. "Closer, closer. Closer still." They beckoned until she was on her hands and knees with her ear close to their petals. "You're ugly!" they would finally tell her, and laugh in shrill unison.

At first, Mrs. D was mad at these vain flowers, and she would refuse to acknowledge them for days, although she never withheld water. The flowers would cajole her back, complimenting her in a way that made Mrs. D doubt their sincerity, but she found herself lured back to them nevertheless. They were so lovely, and maybe they were right. She knew she was no beauty, was short and squat with deep lines like a puppet around her mouth, so she forgave them for their honesty. She would unfold a lawn chair and sit beside them, listen to them chattering. She had no friends here to talk to. She didn't know the language well enough to have made any. There was only Georgie, and he was busy with his own life. Mr. D told her to keep quiet most days because, he said, she annoyed him with her noises. There were days when she didn't utter a single word.

The primroses reminded her of the women back home who, after all the chores had been done, would sit on their stoops and gossip with each other. The flowers had opinions about the neighbours. The Mrs. in the house with the cherry tree wore her skirts too short. The Mr. in the house with the yellow door laughed too loud. When the flowers were good friends, they were very good friends. But the flowers had sharp tongues, and they couldn't resist criticizing Mrs. D after a spell. Eventually, Mrs. D let it all go and tolerated their meanness because no one else on the block spoke Portuguese. The flowers, emboldened, began to dole out their wickedness as matter of fact. "Mr. D hates you. Georgie too."

Mrs. D took all of this in, sitting near them in her garage with its door slid open, watching the neighbours as they walked by. Inevitably, the weather would shift, and the flowers' voices would grow silent as the season cooled, and their petals would wilt and fall to the ground. Did Mrs. D feel some sense of poetic justice when she saw their bare stems? She did not. Instead, she sighed, folded up her lawn chair for the season and thought she would miss them through the fall and winter.

When the flowers arrived in June this time, they went after Mrs. D with a vengeance, without even pretending to be friends. Every morning, they wailed for their water and care, and she gave it to them. This day was the same.

After she recoiled the hose and was filled with satisfaction that she had completed her duty, she went for a walk around the neighbourhood. Some people waved as she passed. She had grown accustomed to their ways, as they probably had in turn become familiar with her shuffling by in her drab dress and head scarf. She had seen them come and go from their doors, their cars, had seen their kids pouring out into the street to play. They were good people, she had decided. She didn't know names or particulars, but she knew.

She walked in circles, up one street, crossed, and down the other side. She may have walked for a couple of hours and said hello once to everybody, nodding on her second and third round. No need to repeat herself. She walked and looked at the ground. She walked and looked at the sky. The sun was blazing today although it was only June. Mrs. D felt the sweat gather at her brow, and she wiped it away with her sleeve. She walked and looked at the young crabapple trees that lined the road. Their pink blossoms were now gone, replaced by hard green leaves that looked like plastic. She knew the small sour fruit would start to grow soon. When she had first moved to this neighbourhood, she picked these apples and ate them until Mr. D told her that here people didn't do that. It made no sense to her for food to grow only to fall to the ground and rot.

When she was young, Mr. D had lived down the narrow lane from her family home. Her brothers used to fish with him at the marina. They said he always got the best catch. Too good to bother with poles and lines, Georgie's father, at nine years old, made a spear from bamboo, sharpening an edge with his pocket knife.

The first time, the other boys swarmed around the beach and watched him as he concentrated like a soldier and dove into the waves, an orange buoy tied to his ankle. The water would have been freezing, but it didn't seem to bother him. After an hour, when capped men smoking cigarettes joined the boys, he returned bearing a huge silver fish that he held by the gills, its side bloodied from a hole that the spear had made. A cheer erupted from the small gang of boys and men, and it had felt like a hero's welcome. The women heard the cheering, and they rushed out with the girls to see what was happening. She was too shy to look at him, so she kept her head down and concentrated on his big toe, which was smeared with drops of blood from the fish. The nail was split in the middle, she remembered. Then some time later, he went away, made a home in this soft country and came back to take her with him. She went, and everybody was happy. Except her mãe. Mãe had stood at the door and said nothing and did not smile. Mrs. D thought about this for a long time, and in a moment of clarity, she wondered if perhaps her mother knew that this man who took her was not just brave, but that somehow, he was also cruel.

A s she continued to walk, she thought about the letter that she received two days ago. It had come in a thin white envelope, and her name had been handwritten on the front. This was a rare thing, handwriting on an envelope. Mrs. D had taken it to her kitchen and carefully used a butter knife to cut the edges so she could take out the neatly folded page. Her brother's scrawl was difficult to make out. When she read his words, that Mãe had been ill for weeks but had finally died peacefully in her sleep, she felt the familiar wind rush through her. She smelled clean laundry, the kind that could only be created by the alchemy of salty wind and sun.

She circled Clara Street until Georgie called her in. He yelled, "Mãe," from the driveway, waving his arm. She looked up and saw her Georgie boy. She was often surprised that he was no longer a baby, even taller than his father. He was so beautiful with his brown curls, like an angel. Even as a baby, he was, she knew, an angel lent to her. The flowers looked up at him too. They smiled and swayed their petals. At fifteen, he had become such a handsome man. She watched Georgie running over to her, and she stumbled as she went to meet him. She wondered, *Will he miss his mãe?* He held her hand and took her home. As they passed, she could hear the flowers hissing at her, impatient. It was time to go, they insisted.

She was tired and wanted to lie down, but her son wanted to make sure something was on the table before his father came home. Georgie was kind. Georgie loved her. He got out the pans while she unwrapped some ground beef from the refrigerator. It came from the store already packaged and weighed exactly one pound. Everything here had a place—a perfect place where things fit into one-pound packages.

Mrs. D heated up some rice and mixed it with the ground beef and some peppers. She left it in a pan and covered it up. She went upstairs to her room to lie down. In her bed of starched linen, she dreamt. Her mãe. Small brown hand over hand to clip the sheets across a clothesline. Large looming clouds and the wind blowing the tall grass. The whites of hydrangea.

She woke up to the sound of the TV downstairs. She went to Georgie's room, but he wasn't there. Down in the living room, she walked past Mr. D in his chair. He was drinking beer and didn't look up. She didn't know if he saw her or if she was already a ghost. She knew this could be true as much as flowers could talk. She looked forward to being invisible. She would be a speck of lint on Mr. D's big split toe while he watched TV. She would be a brown speck on his brown toe against his brown recliner in that brown room.

She stood for a moment in the corner, looking at the back of his head, noticing the large bald patch in the middle. She remembered when it was full of glossy brown curls like Georgie's. It was the curls that had made her think

31

that maybe it would be okay to follow him across an ocean despite her mãe's doubts. It filled her with sadness now, for the hair that was no more. When he used to roll on top of her in the night, she would risk running her fingers through that hair, the only time such behaviour was allowed. It was as soft as she had imagined, like dipping her hand in a basket of down. She felt tears spring to her eyes for the lost hair.

Before the tears could fall, she let herself out the front door and walked to the garage. She went in and started to close the door behind her. But wait. She wanted one more look at the sky. She opened the door wide enough to glimpse the sky. She looked up higher and saw the moon. Bright, bright orange moon. One flower woke up and scowled at her. "Go back to sleep, *sonolenta*," Mrs. D whispered, and winked at it.

This was not the way she would have wanted to die. She would have preferred to lie down in a shallow river, her bare back pressed against flat pebbles still warm from the sun, her hair like branches of a tree fanning out from her head. She wanted to face the sky and her eyes to be covered with sunlight that glinted on the water.

She ducked back inside and kept the garage open a crack for the moonlight to crawl through. She retrieved the bottle of bleach from the cabinet at the back of the garage, sat down on her lawn chair, unscrewed the cap and lifted the bleach to her lips. She took a long sip, swallowed, and closed her eyes against the moon.

Fences

When Francesca and her new husband, Nick, moved to Scarborough from downtown, she knew she had entered a world very different from their own. People here didn't have jobs where they sweated and came home trailing dirt. The people here dressed in pressed shirts and slacks, climbed into cars and drove away to air-conditioned or well-heated offices. She worked hard to iron Nick's clothes so that they blended into this landscape.

Francesca was shy about meeting these new people, but Nick, as a car salesman, said it was good to socialize with the "mangia-cakes." They upgraded their cars constantly instead of driving them into the ground like the Italians with their work trucks downtown. Nick saw the opportunity for commissions to be made. Everybody in their old neighbourhood was proud of them for rising from the construction sites that their fathers toiled in to a job that allowed for soft hands and a new place in the suburbs. It was only a one-hour ride on the bus and subway away, but it may as well have been on the other side of the world.

There was one thing that was reminiscent of the old block where they were from: the children teeming on the streets in packs like bandits. The sounds of laughing, fighting and stampedes of running feet were the same. The adults, though, felt foreign. She made an effort for Nick's sake, and smiled at the neighbours and made tentative steps by accepting their invitations to barbecues and dinner parties, participating in polite small talk while cradling a lemonade or beer. "You don't have to be their friends, Franny. They're neighbours. It's different," Nick said.

Francesca began to notice things about the people on her street. She was particularly interested in the couples. Perhaps because she was a newlywed, Francesca searched for signs of love between married people, noticing the differences from pair to pair. Sometimes it was the way one person laughed at the other's joke. Or a hum of silence between them told of a communion no one else could be a part of. The immigrant Italian parents in her old neighbourhood had never shown outward signs of affection. She grew up accustomed to their short exchanges consisting of women's complaints and men's grunts. But in between, there were moments that she knew were as poignant as a kiss. The way her mother used to scrub her father's nails with a brush every night even though she knew they would be full of dirt again the next day after work. Or love was in her father always serving her mother first when they sat down for dinner.

Some couples' love was easy to spot. For example, their neighbours Marilyn and James, an older couple without children at home, acted in unison, as if they shared one mind, one desire. People liked to be around them for their easy simplicity, and when they had cocktail parties, all manner of neighbours from Winifred, Maud, Clara and Samuel Streets would show up. Dancing would always break out. Watching James spin a giggling Marilyn around to the pulsing disco beat of the Bee Gees made it seem that their love was deep and wide, a basin into which they'd fallen and happily occupied.

Other couples' ropes had frayed. The Bevises, for example, were not in love. Francesca could tell by the way Anthony Bevis stiffened slightly every time his wife, Janine, drew near. These little things may not have been discernible to others, but they were clear to Francesca. She wished she didn't notice, especially when it seemed something more sinister or sad lay below the surface. But she had the ability to see even when she didn't want to. She had known for a long time not to trust appearances at first glance, and that, eventually, people leaked secrets like a pesky tap. If you only watched long enough, it inevitably dripped.

At the mall, whose halls were flanked by ceiling-high mirrors, she would catch a glimpse of her and Nick when they were shopping and study their image as if through borrowed eyes. Slightly slouching was a big-framed man with a round belly, dark curly hair framing a squarish face that held a bulb of a nose, a wide mouth, and saucer eyes. His broad hand easily held her small one, his head tilted toward her. She squinted to determine whether that meant he was attentive, in concert with her will and desire. That she, this woman who came up to his breast pocket, with the shiny brown hair and dimple in her crooked smile, was the other side of his coin. His love.

Try as she might, Francesca could not look at herself in the mirror and objectively see if the woman reflected there was in love. When she'd catch her own eyes, she'd feel startled, as if she were an animal spotted by a hunter. But she looked, always hoping to see that telltale sign that this thing she sought and craved existed between these two people.

When they had first gotten engaged, Francesca and Nick stole every moment they could to duck into her basement to fool around. Her mother was always home, but luckily the floors in their old house squeaked, so if she came close to the basement door, they had enough warning to spring apart. They became adept at making love with their clothes partially on, so they could button or zip them up in a second. The sex was not exactly the stuff of romance novels. The old loveseat was scratchy and lumpy, but Francesca would lie on it as best she could, her calves and feet hanging over the armrest. Nick, with only his fly open, would anchor a knee on either side of her hips as if bracing himself to heft a heavy load or weld iron. Before they would start, they would make out furiously. Nick was a great kisser, and Francesca was always too jealous to ask him how he had learned. He would push his tongue into her mouth forcefully, more forceful than any other act that ever came from Nick. He rolled his tongue across her teeth and thrust in to meet her tongue. These kisses, coupled with his hand squeezing her breasts through her clothes, made Francesca delirious. She couldn't wait until he was inside her and would yank on his zipper to get him to enter her. She always wore a skirt when he was coming over. This made things much easier.

The first entry was the best. She loved the feel of him filling her, pressing at that need. Then after a few minutes, her passion would wear off, even as she felt Nick's build. She didn't know why, but it quickly started to feel like nothing at all and her mind would be brought back to the absurd scene of them on the lumpy, scratchy couch, Nick pumping up and down like he was doing push-ups on top of her. Afterward, they would mop up with the Kleenex that Francesca had the foresight to keep in the basement.

After marriage, they had the luxury of letting their naked bodies press together in their big, wide bed, unrushed. She loved mornings best. She would look at every inch of Nick's body in the slats of light coming through their vertical blinds. She ran her fingers through the soft hair that gathered on his chest. She licked the saltiness of his skin and teased him until he would throw her down and make love to her. It was better than the basement sessions, but she could never sustain the initial sensations. After a few minutes, she would go through the motions, arching her back to feign desire, moaning when he did because it seemed the thing that would bring them together.

When Nick got the job in sales at the VW dealership in Scarborough, Francesca's mother sold their old house and gave them the money to buy a new one. Her mother was satisfied with their move to the suburbs as her job well done and moved back to Italy to live with her sister until news of a grandchild would herald a return.

Nick and Francesca vowed they would have a house with wide windows with glass so clear and clean, you wouldn't even know it was there. The sun would pour in and illuminate the rooms from all sides. Nick and Francesca would not have a constant battle against dust, leaky roofs and loud neighbours like their parents did in their homes downtown. Their future was heading in another direction.

Their home was like arms held wide open. She could have done cartwheels in their living room. At first, Francesca was fastidious about keeping things up. She used lemon Pledge to polish the dining room table every day, sometimes more when she saw a smudge left by Nick's elbows or a sprinkling of dust. She would inhale the citrus fumes with satisfaction after seeing her woody reflection on the table's surface the way the woman in the commercial did. She was also very proud of her vacuum cleaner. It wasn't the fancy Hoover, but it was an Electrolux and it cleaned just as well. Her mother had never had one, nor did they ever have a carpet. Francesca's carpet was a plush cream colour, and she savoured the feel of her toes sinking into it like sand. Unlike the tall, creaky Victorian houses full of drafts that she and Nick had grown up in, this house was brand new and welcomed them as its first-ever inhabitants. Francesca felt that as its first, they had a responsibility.

As soon as they moved in, Nick got his uncles and dad to come over and help erect a fence around their property. Chain-link fences were springing up all over the neighbourhood, so it seemed the thing to do. The five-foot-high interwoven wires, green as if they were meant to blend in with the grass, were ugly to Francesca. They cut into the newly laid lawns, cheapening the scenery of what would have otherwise been open fields between the houses.

She took Nick aside while his father and uncles worked. "Do we have to?"

"Trust me, Franny. Fences make for good neighbours." He kissed the top of her head. "This won't be like downtown, with everybody all in our business. Here, we can still see the neighbours, talk to them, but at the end of the day, that's your side and this is mine." She thought he had a point. Their childhood was filled with neighbours who did not have such boundaries and, like it or not, spilled onto each other's porches and lives with solicited and unsolicited advice and gossip. Privacy was a luxury that they could now afford.

They had wanted to have a baby immediately, so their nightly ritual became dinner, a shower for Nick, some TV, and then sex with the night table light on. By the sixth month, their nightly romps began to mimic the basement episodes. They didn't fully remove their nightclothes, and Nick fell asleep right away and woke up only to his alarm. There wasn't time for cuddling and talking anymore. She accepted this as something that happened when a marriage progressed. She wrote her mother that she loved Nick but that she didn't feel this way every day. There were days when he came home, popped open a beer and fell onto the couch to turn on the TV like she wasn't even there. In these moments, she didn't love this person. Other days, he made her laugh by pretending to enjoy the dinner she'd burned, to make her feel better, and her chest expanded with gratitude. Her mother wrote back and asked what good was love? Nick was a man who could provide. That was enough.

After a year in the new house, they settled into an unspoken routine: She cooked his mother's chicken cacciatore on Tuesdays, and they made love on Friday and Tuesday nights. Monday night was reserved for TV and the big game, and Nick still asked Francesca for her opinion on the plays, the same as when he'd been the fullback on the high school team. That was what initially endeared him to her. He cared what she thought.

The baby was to complete them, round out their happiness. Children were supposed to come and fill the house, which felt half-empty despite how Francesca arranged and rearranged the furniture.

H er life was falling into place as she'd imagined it would. But when a baby didn't happen, she started getting the shakes again. In her parents' house, when they used to come on, Francesca would lock herself in the upstairs bathroom and eat toilet paper until she calmed down. Perched on the edge of the old porcelain tub, she would stuff torn pieces of paper into her mouth, chewing and swallowing until her heart slowed to normal.

It was an event that happened shortly after her father's death that triggered the first shakes. Francesca had come home early from school with a headache and had expected to see her mother in the living room or kitchen. She wasn't there. Francesca heard soft sounds like a shoe shuffling on the floor coming from upstairs. She climbed the wooden steps, gripping the banister because she was beginning to feel faint from the headache. The sound grew louder and came from her parents' bedroom. Francesca pushed the door slowly open and saw her father's best friend, Mr. Rossi, at the edge of the bed, between her mother's spread legs. His brown work-worn hands held on to her mother's thighs, fingers sunk into the flesh like fresh snow. Her mother's black skirt was up around her waist, and her slippers were still on her feet. She watched Mr. Rossi push against her mother and heard sounds from her mother that she didn't recognize. Like a kitten crying. One of the legs of the bed scraped against the floor, back and forth, back and forth.

Francesca walked slowly and quietly downstairs, outside, into the backyard and to her father's work shed. It was her father's domain, full of grease and tools. There was a roll of toilet paper that her father had kept around to wipe his hands, his mouth, spills, anything. Francesca grabbed it and stuffed pieces into her mouth, chewing, swallowing. She could not explain why she did it. It seemed the only thing to do because her mind held no words that could make sense of what she witnessed. She never saw Mr. Rossi and her mother together again, and she never mentioned it to anyone.

From that day, something like a tornado, swirling and thickening, began to build inside her. Her body shook with its force. Francesca was afraid it would exceed her body and pour out of her, wreaking violence on everybody around her. She no longer trusted her mother. Every night when her mother prayed with her rosary, Francesca would watch her fingers move across the beads and feel the storm rising inside her. The image of her mother like an animal, pushing against Mr. Rossi's grunts, disgusted her. This disgust was mixed with a kind of titillation that shamed her, and she pushed it deep down. She would escape to the washroom and eat the toilet paper like Communion, her body like an earthquake.

Once, her mother had found her in there, sitting on the cold tiled floor beside the toilet. Her mother had rushed to her, held her like a baby, rocking back and forth with words of comfort. Francesca felt like it was a movie, this scene of the mother cradling her crazy daughter and calling to the Virgin for help and protection. It felt like someone else's life. Her mother's wails both ravaged and cheered her. She never asked Francesca why.

Once Francesca married Nick, she let her mother believe that she'd healed. Her mother had told her not to tell Nick about the shakes. He wouldn't understand, she said, pressing a finger to her lips. But when Francesca felt the familiar panic close in on her, dashing to the bathroom, sitting on the cold porcelain and grabbing at the paper to put into her mouth was the only way she knew to quiet her mind and make the tremors stop.

That April, a bite of winter still in the air, new neighbours moved in next door. From her front window, she watched the movers unloading their truck, and from the looks of their belongings, Francesca knew the new people would be different from everyone else on their street. Most everyone got their furniture from Sears or Simpsons, but these people's items made for a strange collection: antiques—an old, heavy-looking wood desk and a matching chair on wheels, wood bookshelves with glass fronts, and a giant globe on its own stand. Meanwhile, their other things looked very new and very expensive, like the top-of-the-line Hoover. Francesca knew it was top of the line because a salesman had come to the door trying to sell her one—for forty dollars! Finally, the family pulled up in an old Volkswagen van and parked crookedly between two remaining ice mounds on the street. She made a mental note to tell Nick that these people would probably be in the market for a new vehicle.

A blond woman with tanned arms emerged from the passenger side, wearing a tight mauve V-neck T-shirt and bell-bottom jeans. How in the world did she get such a tan in April? She was thin in the Farrah Fawcett way—long and lean but with ample breasts that bounced as she made her way to the front door, a baby on her hip. She walked with the confidence of someone who was accustomed to having a lot of people make a fuss about her looks. A man stepped out of the driver's side, raised his arms and stretched. His moustache and shaggy brown hair that reached past his ears reminded Francesca of Robert Redford in *Butch Cassidy and the Sundance Kid*. The two of them looked like they could've been from Hollywood. Francesca strained to see if they had California plates, but the van was angled away from her.

A few days later, Francesca spoke to the husband for the first time. She was sitting on her porch on one of the first warm days with a supermarket romance novel. He walked out of his front door in bare feet with the baby in his arms and pointed at the air with his chin. "Nice day, huh?" he said, grinning at her from his porch.

"Yes, it is!" she hollered back, surprised by the volume of her voice. She crossed her arms awkwardly and half closed her book, hiding the garish cover of *The Forbidden Valley* with her hand, not sure how to continue the conversation but knowing she was supposed to.

"What's that you're reading?"

"Um . . . this?" She flipped the book to look at the cover as if she didn't know. She was embarrassed by the illustration of a man crushing a woman to his chest. "It's something a friend lent me. Silly."

He strode up her walk, hand extended. "Paul Willis. Just moved in with my wife, Cheryl, and our baby girl, Megan." He hoisted the baby with thin, blond hair standing on end like a crown.

Francesca took his hand, noting the firm grasp, the light hair on his arm and the lopsided smile. "I'm Francesca. My husband is Nick. Welcome to the neighbourhood. Hello, Megan." She gave the baby's hand a little squeeze.

"*Francesca*, eh? That's pretty. I think I'm going to call

you Frankie, though." He winked. Francesca blushed and hated herself for it. She raised the book to her face to hide.

"I bet I can write those . . ."

She brought it back down and blinked, not understanding.

"Those books. Those romances. I bet I can write those and make a million bucks too."

"Oh . . ." She hadn't expected that.

"I'm a writer." He shrugged. "But nothing like that garbage. I'm a struggling schmuck of a writer. But shit, maybe I should knock out some of those romance novels and use a pen name . . . Ha! Sorry, I didn't mean to offend your taste in literature. I'm bitter. I've been trying to finish a novel that will likely be read by ten people." He smirked at his own self-deprecating humour. The baby began to squirm. "Better get in; it's time for the morning nap." He stroked the baby's buttery arm. "See you, Frankie. Good meeting you."

Over the next weeks, Francesca took to bunching her sheer curtains together in her fist and standing behind them to spy on the Willises. Paul was around a lot, either sitting on the porch or coming back and forth from walks or the store with Megan in a stroller. Francesca was too afraid to talk to him again because she could feel heat rise from her neck and creep up to her face. There was no reason; he hadn't been very charming or even interested in her as a person, let alone anything else.

On weekends, Cheryl was also home. She mentioned to Francesca that she worked as a copy editor in an advertising firm and wanted to become a creative director. Francesca had pretended she knew what that meant, but she had never met anyone in advertising before, let alone one that looked like Farrah Fawcett. Even on Cheryl's days off, with her messy ponytail and bare face, she still looked like she'd walked off a magazine spread. Francesca would furtively glance at Cheryl's long legs and the perfect cleavage dotted with freckles peeking out of her V-neck T-shirts. One warm May day, Nick was grilling at the barbecue and began chatting easily with Cheryl and Paul over the fence while they frolicked with their child. Francesca tried to look busy, running in and out of the house to fetch condiments and plates and napkins.

Each time she appeared, Nick would try to include her in the conversation. "Franny, guess where Paul and Cheryl lived? On Beverley Street when they were going to college." He turned to Cheryl. "That's just around the corner from our old 'hood, where we both grew up."

"Really, Nick? We loved it there. It was so authentic!" Cheryl made a wistful face. Francesca wondered what she meant by "authentic." Nick smiled.

"Yeah, we loved doing our grocery shopping in Kensington Market," Paul added.

Nick brightened. "Did you ever go to the chicken place on Augusta? You know, in the market? My uncle Luigi owns it."

47

"Oh, we're vegetarian, Nick. I always felt so sad for those chickens."

Francesca looked at Cheryl, who shook her perfect head and bit her lower lip ever so slightly. She certainly did look sad, Francesca thought.

Nick flipped their steaks. The grease sizzled on the grill. Francesca knew he was very proud of Uncle Luigi. The whole Italian community got their chickens and eggs from his store. She felt embarrassed, but then she was confused about whom she was embarrassed for. She headed back inside to get some salt and pepper even though they normally didn't bother with extra seasoning. While she was gone, Paul turned on the sprinkler. She returned to see the three of them running through it, howling with laughter, while Nick chuckled and called them a bunch of grown kids. Cheryl and Paul with Megan between them were leaping through the strings of water until their clothes clung to them. Cheryl's hard nipples and Paul's chest hair pressed against the thin fabric of their shirts as they all tumbled together on the grass. Tiny rainbows formed in the water around them.

Francesca's interest in her neighbours shifted. She replayed their conversations in her mind throughout her days as she vacuumed, mopped and cooked Nick's dinners. Innocent encounters on their front lawns or in their backyards, talking about the weather, would merge with her imagining running her hands over Paul's chest or up Cheryl's long legs. In the middle of the afternoon, she would take long hot baths, her legs straddling the faucet, trembling as drops of water hit her. In her fantasies, she was never herself, but Cheryl. She was leggy, full-breasted and tan with tumbling honeyed hair, quaking from Paul's tongue between her legs. In her thoughts, they were entwined, like legs, like lips, like passion.

Her body never felt satisfied, and her chest would feel hollow. She would rock herself in the water that had grown cold, feeling shame for how she'd run her hands over her own body, for the state she'd just moments before been in, and repeat exactly one hundred times, "Nick is a good man. I love Nick," before slowly climbing out of the tub.

Her hunger would reawaken in the evenings, when she would curl her fingers through Nick's hair, not caring that it wasn't Tuesday or Friday. She dabbed Shalimar behind her ears. When he turned on the game after work, she sat in his lap. Nick, surprised by Francesca's boldness because she had never initiated sex, would rush her to the bed. They would laugh like they were being naughty children while he undid the buttons of her blouse. But the sex was quick, efficient. Francesca's crotch was wet all the time these days, moist with her thoughts of Paul and Cheryl. Nick would admire that she was so ready, and ten minutes or so later, it'd be over. He would shiver ever so slightly before pulling out of her, drop a small kiss on her forehead, then head to the bathroom to clean himself up. She would stay in bed, trembling and unsatisfied. When he came out, he would look at her and shyly ask if she minded whether he caught the end of the game. In the past, she'd always given him a smile, sat up and said something like "Go get 'em, Tiger," to reassure him all was well.

She still did this, but anger came into her throat now, and she would let it simmer and rise. Along with her sexual need, she'd given shape to that anger, picking fights with him now about small things: taking out the garbage, leaving his socks balled up at the end of the bed. Before, she'd cluck her tongue and say Nick would be Nick. Now, the smaller the thing, the more outraged she became. She reminded herself that this was what married life was like. She tried to calm down with breathing exercises, but nothing worked except eating the paper. Nick started asking her more often if it was her time of the month, which only succeeded in making her start to despise him. The more Nick annoyed her, the more guilt she felt for not being satisfied now that she had everything she ever wanted. Most of all, and perhaps the most damning, she realized she didn't love him enough.

O afternoon in June as she was walking home from the Dominion, hefting her bread and bananas in a paper bag, she saw Paul pushing Megan in the stroller. The sight of him excited her, but then she felt afraid. They were away from their houses, their fences, the things that helped them keep their distance. She fleetingly imagined turning around and walking back toward the store.

Even though it had been a while since they'd seen each other, Paul didn't bother with pleasantries. "I just found out that Portuguese woman down the street killed herself last night."

She felt her stomach lurch and tightened her arms around the bag. She had seen Mrs. Da Silva yesterday walking up and down the street talking to herself.

"And I heard there was another suicide earlier this year. That empty house?"

Francesca was still trying to grasp the death of the poor mad Mrs. Da Silva and trying to steady her balance, fighting the desire to fall on her knees on the sidewalk.

"I guess it's not that big of a surprise." He shrugged. "Existential crisis. It happens in places like these."

Places like these? Her mind tried to register what Paul was saying. What were places like these?

He lit a cigarette and drew on it, and let the smoke escape from the corner of his mouth. "The picture-perfect suburban dream with the groomed lawns, nine-to-five jobs, 2.5-children kind of places. Domino effect. One person decides this ridiculous life is unbearable and utterly boring and then they all fall down." He swept his arm up and down the street as if to explain everything, a contrail of smoke following his thought.

A flash of both anger and awe cut through her whirling thoughts. Who was he that he could gather and explain all these lives in a few sentences, flatten her whole neighbourhood with a simple gesture of his arms? Paul's words and his confidence shocked her even if she didn't completely understand. This life was better than she could have ever dreamt for herself and was certainly more than her mother would have ever expected. It truly was better. Was it happy? Was it so unbearable to be bored? Had Mrs. Da Silva been bored? Francesca gripped the bag of groceries hard until her nails dug into her palm and she felt the pain. She nodded at Paul, pretending she agreed. She wondered whether Paul was bored too, or whether he was above such things.

She felt humiliated to be cast as a part of this group of people he could so easily dismiss, and yet Francesca hoped he saw her as his confidant, someone who felt and thought these big thoughts about others too. She hoped he didn't include her as one of those living ridiculous and meaningless lives. Paul tossed his cigarette on the ground and stepped on it with the toe of his sneaker. When he turned back to look at her, he must have seen distress on Francesca's face.

"Hey, I'm sorry." Paul paused and pulled her against him for a hug, the bag of groceries between them. "Ah, sweet Frankie. I'm sorry if I sounded flippant about it." She felt the muscles of his arms around her and let him hold her for a moment before pulling away. His touch felt like an electrical shock.

◇◇◇◇◇

That fall, Janine Bevis, one of the stay-at-home moms Francesca knew, hanged herself in her upstairs bathroom. The women on the street were divided into two categories: the working moms and the stay-at-home moms. The working moms were always purposeful in their stride between their front doors and cars. They wore makeup and polyester pantsuits and blouses that tied into bows at the collar. The stay-at-home moms wore flared jeans and sneakers. Their hair was lank and dirty, and sometimes their breath stank because they hadn't had time to brush their teeth. Some of the stay-at-home moms looked after the kids of the working moms after school. Despite this overlap, it was a business arrangement, and the two types of moms did not otherwise socialize. There was a general distrust between the two groups of women; each made the other feel a sense of inferiority.

Francesca belonged to neither group. She did not work outside of the house nor have children to tend to. But Janine Bevis had befriended Francesca. Francesca was often embarrassed that Janine would spot her staring out her window, something she did often. Janine always waved and, once caught, Francesca would wave back. Janine began to take this as an invitation to come to the door. They would sit at Francesca's kitchen table over coffee and chat. It was easy to talk to Janine because Janine liked to talk about herself. At first, it was breezy conversation—gossipy tidbits about the other neighbours, Janine's frustration with potty-training her toddler, the weather. But one day, Janine grabbed Francesca by the elbow and pulled her closer and asked, "Can you keep a secret?"

Francesca felt dread. She hated secrets, wished they didn't exist and that everybody could be who they seemed they were without these hidden layers. But she nodded anyway, not wanting to let her new friend down. Janine whispered that she had had an abortion. Francesca had never met someone who had one before. Janine also didn't seem the type. She wasn't some unwed teenager.

Janine quickly apologized to Francesca. "Oh shit, sorry. Here I am going on about this, and you don't even have a child yet."

Francesca said, "No, it's okay."

It was enough for Janine to go on talking. Over many cups of coffee during quiet mornings and with Janine's youngest child napping on the sofa, Janine talked obsessively about it, torn between necessity and morality. She didn't want any more children because she felt they were already barely getting by on her husband's, Anthony's, salary. Anthony was raised Catholic and she knew he wouldn't agree, but she went ahead and did it anyway. Janine was terrified he would find out.

No one else knew, and Francesca didn't know why she was singled out, but it felt good that Janine trusted her. She began to look forward to Janine's visits, which usually came in the wake of another fight with Anthony. Francesca liked sitting Janine down at her kitchen table while her counter and floors gleamed with cleanliness. She took out the coffee pot she had received as a wedding present and kept topping up her guest's mug while Janine gulped from it between sobs. At critical moments, Francesca would reach across the table to enfold Janine's hands in hers. Offering comfort to Janine in crisis made Francesca feel like she was part of something colourful and dramatic.

When there were spells when Janine didn't call on her because things were well at home with Anthony and the kids, Francesca missed her visits.

It was Janine who insisted that Francesca attend the morning gab sessions with the other stay-at-home moms. "What? You have anything better to do or something? Don't shut yourself up in your house, waiting for your man all day." Francesca looked around her at the perfectly polished dining table, the stupid stain beneath the coffee table that would never come out no matter what newfangled carpet cleaner she bought, and realized that Janine had a point.

So, she began having coffee with the stay-at-home moms, surrounded by babies and dirty laundry. They were a nice group, variations of the same theme. "Mangia-cakes," as Nick would call them. They talked about their children, the price of bananas and their neighbours. If there were dirty dishes in the sink, Francesca automatically rolled up her sleeves. If there were baskets of clean laundry nearby, she would fold the children's clothes into neat stacks. Her neighbours teased her for her Italian housewife ways. She would smile and change the subject to the unreasonable price of ground beef.

Shortly before Janine's death, the women had all been talking about the two suicides and Mr. Lems's death a week earlier. Janine had been there like she always was. She'd even had her own theory. "Bunch of losers. All of them. That's what they had in common. Losers who made such shit of their lives that they had no choice but to do themselves in. Finley was a major A-hole, whose wife and kid probably hated him. Mrs. Da Silva let herself go mental. Lems? Alcoholic fuck-up. Their families are better off without them. Everybody is better off without these losers in the world taking up sidewalk space. They should be thanked for self-selecting to exit this planet."

Janine was no shy violet, but she had never spoken like that before. The room was silent, the other women taken aback by Janine's vitriol. While they were not immune to being mean about their neighbours at opportune moments, there was something about speaking of these specific tragedies that left the air thick after Janine's speech. Janine, perhaps sensing this, shifted tone.

"What they needed," she said, leaning back with her arms over her ample chest, "was a good lay to screw their heads back on right."

The other women all had a raucous laugh over that, relieved. They revelled in the brand of humour that was familiar, crossing back into a cruelty that felt acceptable. After all, those who had died had been the outliers, the neighbours who were hard to love, difficult to know: Mrs. Da Silva had never been quite right in the head, and Lems, whether it was a suicide or not, was a fall-down drunk. And Finley was wound so tight, it seemed a no-brainer, someone said, which caused the women to fall into paroxysms of laughter so hard it turned to tears and they used up half a box of tissues. But then a week after this conversation, Janine Bevis was dead. She'd been one of them. She'd been normal.

This latest suicide settled on Francesca like a spider in her stomach. She played Janine's conversations about her abortion in her head and felt the weight of this knowing heavy on her. She became watchful of the others around her, wondering what they felt, what they also hid and who could be next. The stay-at-home moms, who during the school year were each other's lifelines, ceased all gossip and avoided each other's eyes on the street, murmuring a quick hello before hurrying away. Janine's husband and children moved away shortly after her death, and it was as if Janine Bevis never happened.

Francesca wracked her brain for answers. What were the warning signs? What could she have done to help Janine? Could it happen to people like her? Or Nick? All along, this had felt like other people's problems, but now she began to feel as if she could catch suicide like a virus. As if invisible germs could invade and take control of her mind and body.

She tried to talk to Nick. "Babe, don't worry about it.

We don't know what happens behind closed doors. We need to be thankful that we're so happy." He also said suicide was a sin. That it was between Janine and God. Nick didn't cite God too often even though both of them had grown up in the Church. If Nick knew it was two sins and not just one that Janine committed, she didn't know what he would say. He patted her knee like she was a child. She looked at his big, heavy hands and felt the urge to slap them.

The day after Janine Bevis's death, after Nick left for work, Francesca went into the bathroom, sat on the toilet and chewed on a corner of toilet paper. The small spider inside her was growing, gaining traction. This felt different from the usual pressure of the shakes. The shakes would arrive quickly, sweeping her along. This time, the dread grew slowly, stealthily, and could not be relieved with eating the paper. What was happening to her? She had a good life, a wonderful life. She stood up quickly. Trembling, she gripped the banister as she went down the stairs. She rushed out of the house before she could pause to consider why what she was about to do was a bad idea.

She went to Paul's door and peered through the screen. He wasn't in the living room, so she knocked. "Oh, it's you, Frankie," he said as he opened the door. He sounded unsurprised, as if he'd been expecting her. He was unshaven, looked like he hadn't slept, and smelled like he'd rolled in spilled coffee and ashtrays. "C'mon in."

She froze when she saw his face, thinking she shouldn't

be there. She wanted to tell him what she wanted, needed, but there was so much and she didn't have the words to explain them all. She stuttered, "I . . . I . . . I . . . I need . . . I need a measuring cup. I . . ." She felt herself go damp with sweat and realized she was shaking from the effort of uttering words. If he were to ask what she was going to make, she'd have no idea. The small lie already felt huge. He waved her in. "Sure, sure," he said, and turned to lead her down the hall. She took three sharp breaths to try to get the air back into her lungs before following him into the house.

Their house was in disarray, and as they walked through, she instinctively started to pick some toys off the floor, but she didn't know where to put them.

"Leave that. Come have some coffee. The baby's asleep, so we have to be quiet." He disappeared into the kitchen, and she followed, settling the toys quietly back on the floor. She was still trembling and held her hands together for fear of him seeing.

"Sorry, Frankie. It was a rough night. Cheryl and I had a shitstorm of a fight. Didn't sleep at all."

She sat down at the kitchen table covered in ashtrays, newspapers, bills and magazines. The jumble was unsettling. She had always imagined their home to be spilling with sunshine, scented with the smell of wood polish and lemons, filled with art and books. Instead, she found dust clouding in the air and piles of paper threatening to tumble onto the floor. The chaos hanging in precarious balance put her more on edge. She desperately wanted to straighten the debris, throw the cigarette butts into the trash and fill the sink with hot suds. Instead, she sat on her hands to try to keep them still. If only Paul would hold her, she thought, he would be able to stop her tremors.

In the corner of the kitchen, the radio was playing a Billy Joel song. Paul swept aside some of the mess on the table and placed a coffee in front of her. She sipped. A bit of milk, no sugar. She felt warm toward him that he'd assumed how she'd take it. "Are you okay?" She didn't know what else to say.

"Yes. No. Hell, I don't know anymore." He pulled his fingers through his hair, and she wished she could smooth the locks back or stroke the dark shadows under his eyes. "Cigarette?"

She didn't smoke but she nodded. He took two out from his pack and lit one with his lighter. She heard the flame crackle as it rose to meet the tobacco. He inhaled and handed it to her before lighting his own. She took it with her shaking hand, but he didn't seem to notice. She held it awkwardly between her fingers.

"She should have said no before all this happened." He slammed his hand on the table.

"All what?"

"All this bloody mess. The house, the kid." He took a long drag, holding the smoke in his lungs for a long time before letting it explode from his lips. "She said we would travel right after university. We were going to go to Central

America. Ride the chicken buses until we found a place we liked. Leave all this superficial shit."

Central America. Where was that? She hadn't ever heard of anyone wanting to go there, let alone on a chicken bus.

"Then she got pregnant, and God, I love Megan. You know I love my baby, right?"

Francesca nodded. Of course he did.

"But at the time, we were still hooked into our dreams. I asked if she wanted to keep the baby. And she went crazy. For all her pro-choice marches, she went ballistic when I mentioned it was even an option. So we had Megan, but then Cheryl's ultra-conservative parents wanted us married, and Cheryl said we should, that it would make them happy and us a family, and so we did. Then they bought this house for us and gave us her grandparents' heirloom furniture, and it was fucking crazy how easily it all slipped in."

He still looked bewildered as he gazed around at the stacks of dirty dishes, the butter dish with flies swooping around it, the disarray. Francesca thought about her own parents' house, the hours that her father had put in laying concrete long after his body should have given up enduring such work, and her mother, paid by the piece, sewing the heaps of formal gowns that she would never wear in order to save money for the house her daughter would buy some day. Her parents had wanted it more than anything they'd ever wanted, this life. Stability, safety, family. And they worked and worked to make sure Francesca would have it.

Now what? Francesca felt her guilt rise. She heard Janine's voice that day with the stay-at-home moms as a warning. People fucked up their lives and there were no returns. Was this what was happening? Was she digging her own hole of no return? Yet why did she not want to get up and leave this house?

"But I said that I would write. That was the deal, and she agreed. She said she would work. Our lives here would be like fodder for fiction or a great exposé of the middle class. It would be a performance. The more we talked about it, the more fun it sounded."

Francesca held the lukewarm coffee and wondered about Cheryl in her grown-up white blouses and blazers. Francesca envied her for her briefcase, for her husband and child kissing her on the driveway every morning before she drove off. She seemed like one of Charlie's Angels.

"Only it turns out that it's not fun, and it's not okay anymore that she's stuck in the rat race. She wants out, and she wants me to get a job so she can stay home with Megan. It's her turn, apparently. She told me to act like a real man . . . I don't know anymore, Frankie." He stubbed out his cigarette harder than he had to on a plate already full of butts. "I'm so close to finishing the novel!" His head snapped up, and he looked at her as if he'd just noticed her. "You understand, Frankie. Right?"

She couldn't turn away from his eyes and felt her own brimming with tears. As if in a trance, Francesca stood up slowly, took his hands in hers and pulled him to his feet. He rose, his eyebrows arched in an expression of surprise. The linoleum felt cold on her soles, a sharp contrast to the heat coming off the rest of her body. She pulled him close until her T-shirt brushed his hard chest.

"Frankie, are you sure about this?"

She didn't answer. The song "Me and Mrs. Jones" was playing, and he swayed, one hand holding hers and the other encircling her waist. Francesca realized that she was holding her breath. Her feet lifted slightly, one at a time, and she let herself press her face to his shoulder. His smell was different up close, Sunlight laundry detergent layered over sweat.

Her despair rose to the surface then, sharp and cutting. Here was what she wanted: a heated, churning, messy life held inside a kitchen that was an exact replica of her own but completely different. She wanted to keep this surge that lifted from her heart to her skin, the tingle through her muscles. She thought of these things as he danced with her, handling her like she was fragile. The space that she now knew would never be filled by her own life opened up like a hole at her feet. They danced, and she turned her face to his warm neck, aching to feel the pulse of his vein beneath her lips.

He took her right in the kitchen, leaning her against the table. He lifted her skirt and pulled down her underpants, his lips locked on hers. She felt like water under his hands. Before thinking, before words could form in her brain, he was already entering her. He wasn't gentle anymore, and she welcomed his roughness, his taking. She raised her body to his and pushed against him equally hard. They were purely their biology, their instinct, and for once, she didn't wonder at the strangeness of this act. She heard the sounds she made, and they were not calculated moans but sounds that escaped from the tight, dark place of her being as it opened. She didn't know what feeling was rising inside of her, but then she exploded, her voice loud, calling.

He told her to open her eyes and look at him. When she did, she met his eyes. He looked at her unlike anybody had ever looked at her before. He was hungry. She reached for him again to make him return to her, harder now. Behind half-open lids, with her head on the table and hair in the ashtray, she also saw behind him and through the glass sliding doors of the kitchen. She saw the side of her house, the lace curtains of their kitchen window, above the sink. She had sewn those curtains herself, picking the material carefully from Fabricland. She had loved washing the dishes and gazing out the window through that pretty lace. But more than the brick of the house and the lace framing the window, she saw the green wire fence separating here from there, and she squeezed her eyes closed again and felt Paul inside her, jerking her body back and forth, and she wanted it.

After a long string of music, the radio announcer cut in with a commercial, and in that one second, he let her go. She didn't know if he'd finished, but he was suddenly zipping himself into his pants. A baby's low wail was coming through the wall. She got off the table and stumbled backwards, knocking over a chair. She pulled her underwear up from around her feet. Her heart was racing, and she felt everything was slow and fast at the same time.

Paul did a little hop as he did up his button. She scrambled, trying to regain her footing, but felt herself unable to quite get up.

"Isn't this what you wanted? You've been looking at me for months, Frankie." His voice was neither kind nor cruel.

Her face burned with heat. Yes, she did want it. She wanted it again. She resisted getting up and pulling him back into her. She wanted to taste him this time. Francesca wanted him to fill her. She wanted all these things even as it disgusted her. She finally lifted her eyes toward him. She thought his eyes showed pity and maybe regret. She stumbled to her feet then and bolted to the door, racing down the paved walkway and running into her own house. She dashed into the bathroom, slammed the door shut and locked it. She grabbed the toilet paper, turned and sank to the cold tile floor, ripping at the paper and putting the pieces into her mouth as her nose ran and mixed with her tears. She ate through several sheets, then turned and vomited the white mass into the toilet. She waited for her breath to steady, went into her bedroom and fell onto her perfectly made bed.

That was how Nick found her when he returned from

work. She felt a hand on her cheek and woke to see him above her, the room dark.

"Shhhh. It's okay. Sleep."

In her haze, she wondered why he was handling her with such compassion before she slipped back into sleep. She smelled of cigarettes and another man. When she finally awoke, the clock on her bedside table read one a.m. She felt next to her and the bed was empty. She stood up and realized she was still in her clothes. She went to the bathroom to rinse her face. Horrified, she saw the shreds of toilet paper on the floor. Did Nick see? She hastily grabbed them all with her wet hands and wadded them into a ball, throwing them in the garbage can. She plucked off the pieces of paper from between her fingers and went downstairs.

Francesca found her husband sitting in the dining room with paperwork spread across the table. He looked up when he heard her come down the stairs.

"Hey, sleepyhead."

"What are you doing up, Nick?" She held back.

"I brought home some work. The boss said he would pay me extra if I took on a bit of the accounting. It's not hard, just tedious. But I thought if I did this, we could have something extra to take a trip somewhere. You said you wanted to go to Florida maybe, right?"

She nodded and stared at him for several long seconds. He smiled up at her from his chair. His face looked tired. But it was right there, in his eyes. He loved her. Francesca took quick steps to him and wrapped her arms tightly around his neck from behind. He caressed her arm and bent his head to kiss her hand. He would keep her safe forever if she let him. In exchange, she would keep him safe too. This was her marriage and her vow.

She would seal her secrets in a tight box and never open it again. This was what everybody did, she now understood. Her mother, Janine, Mrs. Da Silva, Paul, Cheryl, maybe even Nick. Every day presented choices to be made, who to love, who to be. Every day was a collective staring down into a deep hole of one's own making and imagining. Having come close to the edge, Francesca decided she would pull herself away. From now on, she would only live on the flat surface where the light caught everything, reaching even the corners.

Treasure

Marilyn was a thief. This was as true as her hair was auburn (now striped with grey) and she was tall. When she was younger, she would take this aspect of herself and hold it to the light like a marble, and turn it over to examine it. She used to wonder why she was a thief, and when no answer seemed forthcoming, she stopped wondering.

Marilyn was acutely aware of the thrill that thieving gave her from the first time she took a tube of lipstick from the purse of her beautiful best friend, Lucille, when she was sixteen. She remembered being fixated on the pink tube edged in gold. The colour was called Lilac Memory. It was a ghastly shade on her friend and yet Lucille treated the lipstick like it was a magical wand. Lucille was the kind of beautiful that the ugly lilac enhanced. It made people pause to look even longer at her and ponder that even with that clash of colour, Lucille was a riotous beauty. Marilyn was, as she would be her entire life, merely a sidekick. Her friends were always the prettier, the funnier, the smarter, the more interesting. And when she was alone, no one noticed her at all despite her height.

Marilyn found that for weeks before she took the lipstick, she was always aware of where it was, painfully attentive to Lucille's careful application of the garish purple on her lips and the return of it to her purse's inside zippered pocket. Several times a day, this act was repeated, and so were Marilyn's tense observations. When she finally reached into Lucille's purse and snatched the lipstick, the pounding of her heart, the sheen of sweat that glazed her body lightly and even the sharpening of her vision were delicious, revelatory. She imagined it was as close to feeling like God as she ever could. And so, she continued.

There was always a touch of regret when people noticed what was missing. That first time, Marilyn chewed her nails to the quick as she watched her best friend tear apart her own bedroom in search of that favoured lipstick. The guilt was fleeting. Marilyn found that she was able to inhabit the excitement of the act again and again when she pulled the terrible purple across her own lips or cupped the weight of the tube in her hand. Besides, Lucille had more than enough going for her. She didn't need the lipstick too.

The joy of the conquest and the revelling in her trove never let her down. She perhaps caused some momentary irritation, but real, permanent harm? Never. Most people had too much stuff anyway. Her pleasure, she reasoned, greatly outweighed the crime. Besides, Marilyn knew she was a very good person, and she worked harder to be one. Meanwhile, her collection of pilfered objects grew, and she stored them in hidden boxes under her bed.

A s one of the first people to move into the new subdivision, Marilyn tried to make an impression right away. When other people arrived, she made it her job to welcome them. Her husband, James, was her skinny shadow, following her around with a jovial smile to match hers but with fewer words. Together, laden with paper plates of home-baked cookies wrapped in plastic, they would walk across the dirt lawns, not yet covered by turf.

It was a contradiction, perhaps, given her predilections, but Marilyn thought of herself as a very generous person. She carried herself regally, not stooping her shoulders like other women her age. She was large but not fat. Thick, she would say. She was a formidable figure, and the neighbours quickly succumbed to her sense of purpose and friendliness. When she and James introduced themselves to each new household with the vivacity of teenage counsellors on the first day of summer camp, her sharp eye caught all the details of the neighbours' belongings.

I t only took seconds for Marilyn to assess what she wanted. A small ballerina figurine placed not in the centre of the display cabinet but on the edge like an afterthought. A copper watering can on the kitchen counter. A chipped blue coffee mug left on the porch. It was the little-ness or the copper-ness or the blue-ness of these objects that spoke to her. They had animal qualities, these objects. Marilyn didn't think it was so much her stealing them but their calling to her. She would make silent promises and bide her time.

She and James had moved from downtown and were happy to be in Scarborough and its relative quiet. Both of them were recently retired accountants looking for a place to settle into their twilight years. She loved the neighbourhood's newness. Their two-bedroom bungalow smelled like fresh sawdust and varnish, and the street was stirring with spindly new trees and young families. She always had a biscuit ready to hand to a teething toddler out on a stroll with their parents. This easy generosity made her one of the most popular people on the block, the one whom neighbours went to when they needed to borrow a ladder or a cup of sugar, or to get advice on cooking a roast. And Marilyn was more than willing to preside over the street as its matriarch.

"Marilyn is a treasure," the neighbours would say.

When Mrs. Da Silva died, it was Marilyn who coordinated the efforts to be neighbourly. She went door to door and solicited casseroles from everyone to deliver to Mr. Da Silva and the poor boy, George. For those who hadn't yet heard, she was happy to be the messenger of the grim news.

"That poor Mrs. Da Silva. It was suicide." Marilyn

would deliver the last word in a whisper, her hand floating to her heart. "We all knew she hadn't been quite right, but I *never* thought it would come to this." Marilyn would pause to let the news sink in while she looked up to the sky, the barest hint of tears gathering in her eyes. "Now, let's show our support in this moment of grief. They will *need* things, so if you can cook up something that can be frozen, that would be best."

"Oh, Marilyn. Thank you. You are so good. So kind." One after another, the neighbours praised her, feeling such gratitude for *their* Marilyn.

The day after drumming up edibles for the remaining Da Silvas, Marilyn, followed by a group of women on the street, delivered armloads of Corningware to the Da Silvas' door. Marilyn rang the bell while the other ladies waited on the porch.

Mr. Da Silva opened the door in his undershirt, his face heavy with fatigue. "Mr. Da Silva, we are so, so sorry to hear the news of your wife's death. We all liked Mrs. Da Silva very much." Marilyn scrunched up her face in an effort to be sorrowful. The women behind her nodded like a cluster of macaws. Mr. Da Silva stared dumbly at them.

"Mr. Da Silva," Marilyn tried again, "the ladies and I have brought food for you for the days ahead." She raised the platter in her arms as if to say, *See?*

Mr. Da Silva grunted and moved aside for the women to enter. They couldn't all fit into the hallway of the house, so like an assembly line, they passed the platters forward from hall to kitchen to Marilyn, who then neatly stacked them in the freezer. "There, Mr. Da Silva. All done!" She clapped her hands together. When he didn't move to say thank you, she awkwardly patted his back and said, "Let us know if there is anything we can do . . ."

As soon as he and the other women turned around to move toward the front door, she slipped a pair of scissors that had been on the top of the fridge into her apron pocket. After they filed out, Mr. Da Silva shut the door behind them without even a thank you.

As they walked away, Marilyn shook her head and brightly remarked, "Oh well. Wasn't it the Bible that said love thy neighbour?"

"I guess God hadn't met Mr. Da Silva," said Janine Bevis. The others chuckled guiltily. Mr. Da Silva was indeed very hard to love. Later that evening, Marilyn took out the clothespins that she had stolen from the Da Silva garage last winter and said a silent prayer for Mrs. Da Silva and even the teenager George, who she thought looked like a thug. The clothespins were cheap wooden things, cracked from use. She remembered walking by the Da Silva house one day and, out of curiosity and because the garage door was open, going inside. The clothesline was hanging across it, and pinned neatly on one end was a pretty silk sack. It was bright pink, standing out like a flower against the greyness inside the garage. She had reached into the bag and found these clothespins. Marilyn had thought it was ridiculous that someone would use the refined bag to hold such a stupid thing as old clothespins. But instead of the sack, she pocketed the pins. She didn't know why. She stole by instinct and not reason. There was something about the pins—they were plain but had a vibrancy, a liveliness that was in common with everything else she stole.

After Mr. Finley's, Mrs. Da Silva's and Mr. Lems's death, she rallied the younger people around her at her and James's regular cocktail parties. "Things get bad sometimes. Rocky roads are certainly ahead. But they're part of life. Don't we know it, James?" She would nod in James's direction, and he would answer obligingly, his voice thin and as chirpy as his wife's. The neighbours were baffled and saddened, but their lives weren't greatly disrupted. The dead were not people who got invited to the parties. Still, Marilyn's words pronounced everything that was important to them—family, a home and the spray of sprinklers on grass. Marilyn gently steered them away from the rupture of these deaths and back to safe ground.

"Hold on to each other. That's what will get us through the storms. I don't know why our poor neighbours took the matter in their own hands. I am not judging. Let's hold on to all the good in moments like this. They too will pass." She lifted her Tom Collins and said, "Amen," and all her guests tilted their drinks to their lips after murmuring "Amen."

The suicides caused a bigger agitation inside Marilyn than anyone would have guessed, making her itch to steal more—random things, things that she didn't even want. Instead of adoring them or neatly storing them as she once did, she would cast these objects on the floor of her hobby room with disgust. The more she teetered, the more determined she was to be helpful.

She had got together with James later in life at the plastics company where they both worked in the finance department. She was accounts payable, and James was accounts receivable.Marilyn had grown used to him as a silent man. Days would pass with nothing more than a mention about the weather. Still, Marilyn always placed a cup of hot coffee on his desk at exactly 9:30 a.m. He liked his coffee with two sugars and no milk. After a decade of sitting across from each other, James told her out of the blue that his wife had left him. Marilyn had long committed herself to a life of spinsterhood. She was the one who everybody could rely on to bring the doughnuts in the morning or work overtime while her co-workers had to run home to family dinners. There was something about the way the quiet man looked across at her and announced that his beloved Margaret, the wife who had been packing his ham sandwiches all these years, had left him that made Marilyn see a window.

Being married to the passive James gave her a sense

of calm that she had not known she was missing. Marilyn bloomed. She went from a dowdy wardrobe of white polyester shirts, black skirts and sensible heels to colourful floral pantsuits and sparkly sweaters. She permed her straight lank hair into a frizzy halo around her face. Marilyn even learned to dance, watching *Disco Fever* on television to study some of the moves and making James stand up from his La-Z-Boy to twirl her.

James was a sweetheart, she often told him. He was an easy man, and while he had few words, she made up for it with her cheerful chatter. Marilyn was over the moon when she coaxed a smile from him. She blushed from head to toe and felt like a young girl. She made sure James needed her, taking over anything that required attention—the chores, household finances, the bedroom. For a while, early in their marriage, she even forgot to steal.

Moving here changed that, and she found herself once again on the hunt. Objects beckoned to her from the lawns and living rooms of her neighbours' homes. Maybe it was all the newness, the shiny people. Whatever it was, the neighbourhood gleamed like a field of gems ready to be snatched. Initially, she worried about James finding out, but he seemed fine with accepting the surface of who Marilyn was—a fine woman and wife who made his life comfortable. As long as James seemed content, Marilyn was satisfied.

Most days, Marilyn observed the neighbours from the large picture window in her front room like a mother hawk, her hand always in motion, waving hello and goodbye as people came and went from their homes. Over morning coffee, she would gaze out to the street and speak to James about what she saw.

"James, it's like the United Nations out there! The Portuguese and Italians. And all those Chinese kids. I thought they were supposed to be well behaved, the Chinese. I expect this from the Portuguese and Italians, but the Chinese? They're wild animals! They're known to breed, aren't they?"

Marilyn would shake her head while James chuckled.

There was one kid in particular who made her skin crawl: little June Lee, who came from polite-enough parents, from the limited interactions Marilyn had had with them. But there was something about the way June looked at her, staring at her like she knew things. When Marilyn would step out of her house to collect the mail or shovel the walk, that child seemed to follow her with those small eyes, even in the middle of her childish games. It gave Marilyn the feeling that invisible flies were trying to land on her head.

Secretly, she loathed kids, all kids and not just the Chinese ones on the street. She pretended to coo at the babies, but she was happy she didn't have any. She felt sorry for the Italian girl, Francesca Marino. She saw how Francesca's eyes grew misty when a new baby was paraded around the street. Marilyn felt like taking Francesca aside and telling her the truth: kids were shit and seemed nothing but heartache. But the Italians, Marilyn knew, were more like the Chinese than you think. They loved to procreate like they were going to run out of people or something.

James's grown kids stayed away, probably feeling a sense of betrayal that he and Marilyn had married so shortly after their parents' divorce. Marilyn knew James minded, but if he suffered, he did so silently, like he did all things. And if those children were angry, they also stayed silent like their father. Anyway, who did these terrible children think made their father breakfast, lunch and dinner every day? Washed his stinking socks and stained underwear? Kept the poor man company when he otherwise would not utter a word? Meanwhile, their mother was taking road trips across the country and whooping it up. Really, who should be mad at whom?

Marilyn hid her hoard in the spare bedroom. She called it her hobby room. Marilyn forbade James from ever entering, and James, like always in his life, did as he was told. He assumed it was where Marilyn did all her bedazzling. She was crazy for all that was rhinestones, beads and sequins. All her clothes were embellished with the sparkle, and she offered her services to the whole neighbourhood. For a season, many of the women wore their jeans with bejewelled back pockets.

Unlike the rest of the house, which was orderly and neat as a pin, the hobby room looked like a pirate's treasure cache. Her collection had outgrown the boxes. The newest acquisitions sat on top of the pile while older ones peeped from under the heap. Marilyn liked to spend mid-afternoons here, clearing a spot to sit in the middle of the floor, surrounded by her things. The room and its objects gathered dust that floated sweetly in the air when stirred, surrounding Marilyn like an aura.

One fall day shortly after Janine Bevis's suicide, Marilyn stepped on the highest rung of her kitchen stepladder to get a pan from the top cabinet, lost her footing and fell. She had been feeling shaky since hearing the news. Janine had been a regular at her parties and a loyal follower of Marilyn.

All morning, Marilyn had sat with a pad of paper and pen, trying to summon a good speech to rally her neighbours to higher spirits and meaning, but the words sounded hollow. All she wanted to do was leave her house, walk into all the unlocked doors of the neighbourhood and take. Instead, she tried to distract herself by thinking of the kind of casserole to make for Mr. Bevis and his kids.

The spill startled her, and she didn't make a sound until she was splayed on the floor and a sharp pain in her shin overtook her. "Ow?" she asked in stunned surprise.

At the hospital, the doctor determined it was a proximal tibia fracture. There was talk of surgery, sliding nails, screws and a cast. By now, the pain was fierce and she thought she'd die from it. She graciously asked the nurse for something and was granted an injection of clear liquid. Soon she felt quite comfortable in her hospital bed while James fussed and worried.

"James! My goodness, you're making me dizzy, and I am feeling very fine now. You trust the nice doctors. They'll put me back together in no time."

The doctors and nurses did treat her fine. They treated her like a queen, in fact. Marilyn learned their names, their kids' names and their favourite kind of cookie. "You wait until I get out of here!" she crowed at her orthopaedic surgeon. "I am going to make you the best darn chocolate chip cookie you have ever tasted!" He glowed from her attention.

Back in the neighbourhood, news spread of Marilyn's fall, and the stay-at-home moms spun into action. Their Marilyn was always there for them, and they were determined to be there for her. They instructed James to stay with Marilyn at the hospital while they took care of the rest. One team started cooking up the casseroles. Another mowed the front lawn and weeded the flower garden. Yet another team decided to surprise James and Marilyn and clean their house.

Nobody locked their front doors. Neighbourhood Watch stickers were posted in each of their front windows like badges of honour. Their neighbourhood had not been blemished by a single criminal activity save for the occasional missing items that must have been misplaced rather than stolen. And so, the third team, armed with buckets,

J Cloths and cleaning agents, let themselves into Marilyn and James's house. The house was in good shape, but the women thought they would give it a once-over anyway, to show Marilyn that they cared.

One of them found the vacuum cleaner and got started on making perfect V tracks in the living room. Another aimed for the powder room because she was a believer that the toilet should always be the first thing taken care of. Francesca took the back, passing by the master bedroom first and glancing at the queen-sized bed, the letters *J* and *M* bedazzled on the duvet.

Francesca walked toward the other room. Its door was closed. She remembered Marilyn mentioning that she had a hobby room where she made her sparkling creations. Marilyn had gifted her a set of jewelled placemats once. Francesca eased the door open.

A few days after her surgery, Marilyn was sitting in her bed, watching her soap opera, *All My Children*, propped up with pillows that the nurse named Alice would plump up every half-hour. James entered and sat down, handing Marilyn her favourite jelly-filled doughnut and a coffee from Constellation Doughnuts.

"What took you so long today, James?" Marilyn asked, her eyes not leaving the screen. Erica Kane was going to marry Tom Cudahy today, but she was in love with the Davis fellow. Everybody was already assembled at the church. Marilyn thanked her lucky stars that her surgery did not happen today or else she would have missed this episode.

"Listen, Marilyn. I've got something to tell you." James sat down on the chair beside the bed, wondering how to start. He fidgeted with his hands.

"James, I want to watch this." Marilyn bit into her powdered doughnut, white sugar falling on the pea-green hospital sheet covering her.

"No, Marilyn. We need to talk." He stood up abruptly and clicked the TV off. Marilyn was startled. James had never spoken to her with such authority before.

After the word spread, the news of the thefts overtook the news of Mrs. Bevis's suicide. Some of the neighbours paraded into the Johnson house as if it were an open exhibition. They wanted to see for themselves that Marilyn Johnson was a bona fide thief. To their surprise, nearly everyone who knew Marilyn found things of theirs in her "hobby room" that they hadn't even noticed were missing. A few retrieved their belongings, cradling their various knick-knacks as if, upon rediscovery, the objects had gained new value in their owners' eyes.

"Can you believe it? My garden spade? I mean, it is a good spade. See how it fits in my hand just so? Never had a callus with this one."

Other neighbours left their things in the hobby room as if these objects weren't truly theirs anymore. Marilyn had stolen from them, and yet oddly enough, many didn't feel particularly betrayed. They gazed on the heap—mostly useless things, forgotten things. Assembled in their haphazard way, one on top of the other, as a collective, a mountain of life objects, the items felt substantial, as if their power came from being so unified. The initial tone of outrage shifted. Instead, many of the neighbours began to point out their things with a touch of pride.

"See that napkin ring there? Yeah, under the oven mitt and beside that screwdriver? That's mine. She must have swiped it when she was over for a barbecue last summer."

"There's my fan! I got it as a gift for being in my brother's wife's bridal party. Imagine that! Ha ha!"

Nonetheless, the facts were the facts: the woman they had trusted had lied to them, had taken from their families. They feigned anger, but they were more in awe. The objects themselves were little things, easily replaceable. It was more the double life of Marilyn that triggered surprise. Marilyn, who had comforted them when the suicides happened, had a secret life of her own. They did not discuss the correlation of the deaths and Marilyn's thievery. Instead, they silently nursed their own double selves and worried what they revealed or leaked.

When Marilyn came out of the hospital, she did so quietly. No one went knocking on her door, and James kept the drapes drawn. While some of the neighbours may have had choice words for her, they shared them only with one another and never knocked on her door to say them to her face. She didn't dare go outside. Marilyn sunk into a silent despair, buried herself in sequined quilts and let James take over the household.

James ran errands alone now. People said polite hellos and have-a-nice-days as he went, and to their surprise, James became chatty. He remarked on the weather and the excitement of the city's new baseball team. When he returned home, he filled the house with news of the outside world, and Marilyn, tucked on the couch, listened to his stories about whom he bumped into, the new chili-flavoured Hamburger Helper on the shelf at the supermarket, which neighbour's grass was getting a bit too long and unkempt. His voice, something that Marilyn had never quite gotten used to because she heard it so rarely, became her favourite sound. They settled into a new life, a quieter one, and Marilyn found herself easing into it. Like a retired queen, she let James take the lead and dote on her.

James was gracious enough never to speak of the incident except once. He had been cutting tomatoes to make her a BLT. The bacon was sizzling on the stove, and she bit her tongue instead of telling him to turn on the fan as the kitchen filled with fumes. By then, Marilyn was already fully healed from her operation and walking fine, but James still insisted on her resting and him taking over the cooking duties.

"People may call you a thief, Marilyn, but do you know what you stole?" His back was turned to her while he continued to chop. She was sitting at the kitchen table as the room filled with the smell of fat and the swirl of the smoke from the pan. She held her breath, wondering if this was it. This was the moment he was going to confront her and leave.

"What's that, James?" she asked quietly, bracing herself.

"You stole my damn heart, Marilyn. And I am grateful." He never turned to face her and said nothing else. She listened to the hissing bacon, the rhythmic sound of James's knife on the cutting board, and let out a long exhale.

Days emptied into more days. Things stopped disappearing, but people started to lock their front doors. There were fewer parties and instead of drunken neighbours hollering *Good night* and *Thank you* to each other in the middle of the night, the streets were silent. Now and then, Marilyn gathered the nerve to draw back the curtains a sliver, careful not to be detected. On some of these days, she would see that girl, that little Chinese girl, her eyes directed at Marilyn's shadowy figure, standing on the street as if waiting for her. One day, Marilyn waved, and the girl waved back.

Wheels

The year after all those parents killed themselves, something equally earth-shattering happened: I fell in love. *Ka-boom.*

My mother had warned me it would happen, saying, "June, wait until you are head over heels for a boy!" She said "head over heels" a lot. Mom was also head over heels for Kentucky Fried Chicken, so I never gave it much thought.

I didn't know when or why I first noticed him—he had always been there on the street—but it just sort of happened. Bruce belonged to the Wong family. He was two years older, but he hung out with Josie's brother, Tim, so even though his house was on one of the other sister streets, he was on Winifred almost every day. Before the day I got hit or struck or smitten or whatever you want to call it, I only knew him to be one of the older boys who played hard and fast and high-fived each other and told jokes that made them bend over from laughter. I thought those jokes must have been very dirty.

They did not put up with a younger kid stupid enough not to be able to catch a fly ball or not strong enough to break through the human chain of British Bulldog. They yelled at you and let you know that you sucked, but you couldn't cry. You had to be tough, get up off your bum and get back in the game. If you played well, they'd maybe rub you on the head like a puppy and mutter, "Nice going." Josie lived for those "nice going" moments. As for me, I stayed as far away from them as I could, because their insults and their compliments equally made me nervous.

But then that day happened when he was *really* there in a whole new way, suddenly so bright I couldn't help but see him. He rode by me too close on his bike, the wind snapping at his black hair like a kite. I felt the gust as he shot by, and I turned to look. He was riding standing up, pumping at his pedals, chasing another kid on a bike. He was laughing, and the sound of it surprised me because it sounded like it belonged to a man and not a child. In a moment, he rode past me again, and I could only stare, as if seeing him for the first time. His eyes were squinted toward the sun, his skin was golden and his mouth . . . I noticed his lips, especially his lower lip, plump like a bee had stung it, and my breath caught. I had never thought of boys as beautiful before, but I realized that he was.

On someone's porch, a giant boom box was playing Blondie. The song was about a heart made of glass. They played this song so much on 1050 CHUM that I knew every word, and I had always thought it was a weird song until that moment. I finally got it. I felt like my heart really would fall out and shatter on the road if he didn't look at me. He didn't, not that day anyway, and Debbie Harry's sleepy voice reminded me of how bonkers I suddenly felt.

But it did happen, maybe the next day, or the one after that. Or maybe I gradually appeared to him, emerging from the shadows as a girl-shaped thing. I was only a shred of a pre-woman in training, ponytailed, with dirt under my nails, wearing slightly pink tube socks because my mom was always too distracted to separate the colours from the whites.

Bruce had a bronze ten-speed wrapped with silver, gold and white stripes. He was with it so much, it was as if the bike were an extension of his body. My parents wouldn't let me get a ten-speed, and I felt like a baby on my powder blue Schwinn with its banana seat and plastic orange ribbons trailing from the handlebars. He could pop wheelies in the air, lifting the front wheels off the asphalt like it was nothing. He reminded me of a sparrow ready to take flight as his bike glinted in the sunlight. I remember the other kids cheering and screaming, "Again, again!" I was one of the ones clapping, the short one in the back with my rabbit heart hopping. I tried to pop a wheelie after I saw him do it but fell, the asphalt taking a few layers off my knee. I never tried it again but hung back and watched him.

I was pretty good at all the sports we played on the street, but once I noticed him, I turned into Jell-O. When he showed up, or even if he hadn't shown up yet, I couldn't move or speak or sometimes even breathe. One day that summer, Josie got mad at me when I missed an easy volley during a game. "What's up with you, June? We're three points down!" Josie was very competitive and had always been since the day I met her in Grade 2, when she challenged me to race home from school.

Bruce yelled, "You're not even paying attention, June. You're useless." It was the first time he had ever spoken directly to me and said my name. He was kicking at the concrete, not even looking at me.

Tim said, "Yeah, she's a baby. Go back to your crib, little baby, and don't try playing volleyball." They snickered, and Josie frowned, her loyalty now charged up.

My face grew hot, and I bit my lip to keep from crying. That was the only day in my young history when I went home before the street lights came on. My babysitter, Josie's older sister, Liz, asked me what was wrong when I stomped into the house. I ignored her and planted myself in front of the TV and watched her soap opera. She'd recently turned into a curvy seventeen-year-old, and Josie and I were fascinated by how she would suddenly disappear to go make out with a boy. So far, we had caught her sucking face three different times with Manny, one of the Portuguese kids, in Josie's garage. I would stare at Liz's big boobs, wondering if one day my chest would rise like Pillsbury Crescent Rolls too.

No boys were around this time, and Liz was glued to the TV. All I could think about was Bruce calling me useless. I didn't understand why it mattered to me.

The soap opera was stupid, so I made a mental list of all the reasons Bruce was boring. He went to the Catholic school that was farther down the road on Samuel than ours. Catholic school was for nerds. He was also no different from the other fourteen-year-old boys who did disgusting things like drink Coke and belch the alphabet. Still, he did have a very soft baseball glove that he asked his dad to run over with the car every night to loosen it up, which was pretty cool. And there were those wheelies . . . I tried to think of other things, like how to get my parents to buy me a blue Adidas track suit with the yellow stripes, but my mind kept wandering back to Bruce like a disloyal dog.

Some days later, my friend Nav was over for lunch, and over Chef Boyardee Mini Ravioli, he told me that Bruce had a crush on me, which at first seemed like a mean joke—I liked him, but what were the odds that he'd like me back? I thought about the previous day when he was being a jerk to me. I punched Nav hard on the arm and regretted it right away. He screamed and gave me a hurt look. Nav was not the type to be mean ever. "Sorry, buddy," I said, but my mind was already elsewhere. I finished my pasta quickly and urged Nav to hurry up so we could go outside.

In the crowd of kids, I saw Bruce, his ten-speed balanced against his hip at the curb, staring right at me. He was too bright again, and I looked away quickly, my heart doing that weird skip again. I was worried everyone would see me acting funny, so I ran in the opposite direction, down the street to Samuel and all the way to Mac's Milk. Only when I ran inside and felt the cool air conditioning prickle my skin did I realize that Nav had chased after me. We both waved at Danny behind the counter, like everything was normal, before heading to the freezers. "Yo, kids!" he called to us before putting his head back in his comic book.

"How do you know he likes me?" I whispered to Nav as he followed me down the aisle.

"C'mon, June, he's always looking at you. And before lunch, he asked me where you were." He eyed me. "You like him too," he added.

"No I don't. Don't be stupid, Nav." I pulled out a Creamsicle.

"Your face is red."

"Shut up! I mean it." I spun around, showing Nav my fist and trying to look ferocious, and Nav looked startled and started coughing. I thumped his back. Nav was more like a girlfriend than a boy, a bit delicate and very quiet around most other people except for Josie, Darren and me. When he laughed, he shook like a piece of grass getting rained on. One of my favourite things in the whole world was watching a summer storm with the screen door wide open in the kitchen. I loved the tinny smell of it and especially the drops hitting the blades of grass in the backyard. It was pretty, kind of like Nav.

Sighing, I pulled out another Creamsicle and handed it to him. He nodded and went over to talk to Danny at the cash. Since Nav's parents owned the store, when we were with him, we usually got our stuff for free as long as it was in "good faith." Nav's dad put a lot of stock in good faith.

We headed out and plunked down onto the curb to eat. We slurped at the Creamsicles quickly. It was a hot day, and the orange dripped down our arms.

"What do I do, Nav?" I asked between slurps.

"I dunno. I've never been in love before."

We walked back to Winifred Street, where everybody was deep in a game of Frisbee football. Nothing was out of place, but it still seemed that things were not quite right. Georgie was already at his post in the garage, having been there for a full year since his mother died. He watched the Frisbee fly through the air as the game continued. I felt stupid suddenly that Georgie was there in his garage where his mother killed herself and here I was thinking that I had problems.

On the street, my friends were running hard on the concrete, and multiple hands reached to the sky to catch the disc. In the middle of that mob was Bruce. I couldn't describe his face because I didn't know the words to understand how it made me feel looking at him. Things seemed the same, but I realized that maybe it was me who was different.

The next day, Josie was sent to give me a message. "So . . . Bruce wants to know what you think of him." She had taken me into her garage and closed the door so we could be alone. Wanting privacy was new to us, and as best friends, we felt special when we separated from the others to go talk alone. My eyes took a while to adjust to the darkness. She had her hands on her hips and was popping her watermelon Bubblicious like she was conducting a business deal.

"Why does he want to know?" I asked, trying to sound normal. I picked my shorts out of my bum. My dad said they were too short now and to throw them out, but they were terry cloth and my favourite, so I wore them.

"He likes you, stupid. He wants to know if you want to go around." She kept smacking her gum, talking to me in a tone like she was the adult and I was the child. Josie did that sometimes, making a big deal of being four months older than me. "It's like in 'Mandy.' He feels like that about you." Josie had lately been interpreting all of our experiences through Barry Manilow songs.

"Really?" I asked, sounding like a complete dork.

"I knew it!" she yelped, darting out of the garage to go tell Bruce. I froze, not knowing what to do. The last thing I wanted was to walk out of that cool, dark garage and face Bruce and all of my friends. Everyone would be staring. But I couldn't stay there forever. I left and was temporarily blinded by the sunlight. When my vision came back, everyone was in the middle of a skateboard race down the street and didn't even notice me, already on to the next phase of their lives. From that day on, Bruce and I were considered a couple.

He started by calling my house. I was always the first to answer the phone when it rang since everyone in my family expected it to be Josie. Even though we saw each other every day and lived two doors apart, we still talked up a storm on the phone. My dad called us "the twins."

But when I answered that night with my usual "Josie?" I was surprised to hear that man/boy voice ask back, "June?"

That night, I sat on the kitchen floor, my back against the wall, and had my first phone conversation with a boy. He shot questions at me while I traced the swirly patterns on the green linoleum tiles with my finger. My favourite colour was green. His was blue. My favourite game was snow football, and his was volleyball. My favourite song was Michael Jackson's "Rock with You," and so was his, a fact I privately celebrated. We had something in common! The most important thing was that my best friend was Josie and his was her brother, Tim. Our relationship began to feel comfortably inevitable, like it was meant to be.

Then Bruce asked, "So, do ya like me?"

I giggled and said, "Yes." I made sure not to say it with an exclamation mark because Josie and I had agreed that sounding too excited made boys think you were easy. I didn't know what "easy" entailed exactly, but I sensed that I should not let him know that I liked him too much.

"Do you like me?"

"Yup. Yup, I do, June. I like you a lot." His certainty sent me into hysterics. Did he know about being easy? I put a hand to my forehead to see if I was dying. My face was burning. The phone receiver shook in my hand. "Um . . . thanks," I muttered. I couldn't wait to tell Josie.

The only problem was that the next morning, Josie wasn't interested in hearing about it. I was bursting with information, having replayed the phone call with Bruce a hundred times in my head while I lay in bed the night before, thinking I had a fever because I felt very hot even though a cool breeze blew through my window. I thought about how I would tell Josie—I even practised taking a dramatic pause before saying, "Bruce said, 'I like you a lot.'" But when I went over to Josie's the next day and began with "Guess who phoned me last night?" she looked away, sighed heavily and asked whether my mom had mixed the colours with the whites in the wash again because my tube socks were *ridiculous*. I was shocked; she'd been so interested in me and Bruce, but clearly something had changed. Her disinterest made me embarrassed, so I dropped it and after sitting in her room, helping her fold her family's laundry for a while, I told her I had to go home without even giving an explanation. Before I left, I glanced down at her on the floor, folding her father's giant underwear, and hoped she would tell me to come back and sit down, but she was absorbed with creasing his briefs into a triple fold and didn't even glance my way.

Not having Josie to talk to about what had happened with Bruce sucked all the thrill out of it. I trudged home in a bad mood. It was Sunday, so my mom was home. I found her in the living room, hunched over the coffee table with more forms. She was forever filling out immigration papers to bring her mother from Hong Kong. Mom was always saying, "Any day now!" but she'd been saying it for years. I plopped down beside her and turned on the television. *The Love Boat* was on. It seemed to be a climactic moment during one of Captain Stubing's dinners, but I couldn't figure out what was happening, so I clicked it off. "What's for lunch, Mom?"

"There's no such thing as a free lunch." She didn't even look up from her forms.

"What the heck does that even mean?" I was already annoyed, and she was not helping by offering up more of her riddles.

She paused. "I don't know. But it sounds good," she said brightly. She got up and went to the kitchen. I rolled my eyes. I didn't understand anybody.

That summer, in the evenings after the sun had gone down and I'd had to go home, Bruce regularly hopped my fence to bring me milkshakes from McDonald's. We would sit in my backyard, whispering so my parents wouldn't know that I had sneaked outside. He held my hand, sweaty from his. I didn't like the wetness, but I never said anything, and he didn't either. I wondered if he felt the same way as me. One minute, I would feel cold, and the next, I would be hot. I started to believe that being in love was like being sick. I wished he would kiss me, but he never did. I would stare at his lips, hoping he wouldn't notice.

In the moments between seeing him on the street or talking to him on the phone, all I could think about was him. I replayed our conversations a million times in my head and saved things to tell him the next time I saw him. I wasn't sure if I was doing this right, this girlfriend thing. I began to understand the word *heartache* because I physically ached from the burden of this relationship. I started becoming scared that at any moment Bruce would stop coming with his milkshakes and his hand to hold. Why he came at all was still a mystery to me, and I couldn't figure out what it was I did that kept him coming. I was worried that if I didn't know, I would stop doing it, and he would vanish.

In the cool of Josie's basement one day in early August, a bunch of us were playing Truth or Dare. Darren dared Bruce to kiss me. I was mortified until I glanced at Bruce, and he was smiling and a little red. It was obvious he wanted to. We went onto our knees in the middle of the circle while everybody started chanting, "Kiss! Kiss!"

He took my hands and ducked his face down to mine. I

closed my eyes, imagining we'd hold our lips together until the kids counted to thirty. That it would be soft and sweet and prove my relationship with Bruce would last forever.

But it wasn't like that, or even close. There were a lot of teeth involved and he darted his tongue all around. The others deliberately drew each number out, pausing to giggle and wolf whistle. It was all a little too public and wet to be in any way romantic, but I tried to focus; this was my first kiss, after all. I wanted to remember it always.

When they finally got to thirty, clapping and whooping, my face was wet from below my nose to my chin, and I couldn't look at Bruce. I felt woozy, like I had drunk chocolate milk then turned around and did a hundred somersaults in a row.

I tried to talk to Josie about the shaky-to-the-point-of-wanting-to-vomit feeling that I had all the time. It wasn't necessarily bad or good, and I didn't hate it or like it. But it was something, and I needed to get to the bottom of what that something was. It made me feel scared, to the point where I began to clam up when Bruce came to my backyard. Increasingly, while he tried to keep our conversations going, I said less and less.

Something was going on with Josie too. Every time I tried to bring up Bruce, she changed the topic and told me she had to go do something. The things she said she had to do were stupid things, like go to the store for her mom to buy chicken legs for dinner or clean the bathroom. It was clear she didn't want to talk about Bruce at all. When I finally asked her point blank why she didn't want to talk to me, she said it was because her aunt was very ill. I'd known her aunt had c-a-n-c-e-r, so I backed off, trying to believe that her pushing me away was because of that and had nothing to do with me at all. I didn't want to be a spoiled brat, which Josie sometimes said I was on account of my being an only child.

I tried to talk to Nav and Darren, but they weren't any help. As soon as I mentioned Bruce's name, Darren would throw his hands in the air and say, "Ew. Not your boy problems again, June," and walk away. Nav would shrug and give his standard reply, "I dunno." I missed Josie, but I was also mad at her. C-a-n-c-e-r was serious, but she'd been fine up until it was official with Bruce, and I wasn't buying it. This was what we had talked about forever—having a boyfriend—and now that I finally had one, not only was it not giving me the gushy feeling we'd thought it would, but she'd removed herself, leaving me alone.

Bruce didn't seem to share any of the same squirrelly feelings. He was going more and more public with our relationship. When school started, he would come to my house to walk me to school. I would make him wait for Josie to show up, but when she did come out her door and see us, she'd ignore us and stride ahead. On these walks, I didn't want to talk to Bruce anymore. Once, he even tried to take my hand. It was getting to be too much. I wanted to vomit all the time. I still liked him so, so much, but I couldn't stop the barfy feelings. He still seemed too bright to me, and I couldn't see for all the light. I would walk silently beside him, staring at Josie's back.

"What's the matter with you?" he once asked me on the phone.

"What do you mean?"

"You don't talk to me much when we're out on the street."

I didn't really have a reason. Also, if I were to be honest and say that I felt like throwing up when I was around him, I figured he would be hurt. I wanted to throw up because there was a lump in my throat. That lump made me want to blurt out "I love you!" Would that have made me too easy? Would that have made me barf for real or make me stop wanting to barf? Was that love? Whatever feeling I was having had moved into me with all kinds of luggage, and I didn't have enough room for everything. I was bursting, and I needed some space. So it might have been love, but it wasn't what I had expected.

I started to wish that things were like they were before that day Bruce rode by me on his ten-speed. I wanted to rewind life back to that moment when I saw his face, and my heart could stay intact forever instead of feeling like it was placed on the edge of a shelf and ready to fall off.

◇◇◇◇◇

It wasn't long before Bruce stopped phoning and showing up in front of my door in the mornings. He didn't even come out to Winifred after school as much, and when he did, he didn't say hi. I heard from his sister that he was seeing this other Chinese girl, someone named Linda from way past Mac's on the other side of Samuel. He brought her over once when the leaves were falling off the stunted fruit trees. She was pretty, I thought. She looked very clean. Her whites were white and her darks were dark. She wore a plaid skirt and grey tights under tall red rain boots even though it wasn't raining. Josie and I were corduroy-and-jeans people and never wore skirts. Pretty Linda didn't even play street hockey with us. She sat on the curb and clapped every time Bruce made a goal. He smiled like an idiot at her. Meanwhile, Nav sent sad-eyed looks of sympathy in my direction. I ignored him and pretended I didn't care, playing harder than ever to block Bruce's goals. I dove faster, snarled and leaped on the ball. What I wanted to do was go over to pretty Linda and pull each strand of hair out of her pretty head. How much I hated her surprised me.

At one point, Josie made a slapshot, but instead of aiming it at the goal, she angled her blade, and the muddy tennis ball shot directly into Linda's face. "Ouch!" she screamed. A dirt stain the exact shape of a circle bloomed on her cheek. Linda's hands flew up. Her nails were painted creamy pink, like the inside of a seashell. In a second, Bruce was beside her, asking if she was okay.

I glanced over at Josie, and we shared a look before she yelled over to Linda, "Sorry!" I smiled and then quickly pretended to look concerned. Josie was still the best.

By late fall, things seemed almost back to normal. Instead of Bruce at my door, it was Josie who was there again. We never spoke about Bruce except once, sort of.

"So, I had my first kiss," Josie said while we were walking on Samuel on one of the first days of snowfall. We were trying to catch the flakes on our tongues while we walked.

"What? Who was it?"

Josie shook her head. She wasn't going to tell. I understood that something had changed between us permanently. Where before there was nothing but open space, and I couldn't tell where she began and I ended, there was now a low-lying wall.

"Did you like it?" I asked.

"Hmmm." She wasn't going to answer.

"Teeth, right?"

Josie stopped walking and looked at me without comprehension. I faked a laugh until I really was laughing, and still, Josie stood there looking at me as if I was crazy, and the snow, like giant wads of cotton, kept coming down on us.

Kiss

Josie loved work. Making her own money made her feel like an adult even though she was just twelve. It began with the paper route she inherited from her brother, Tim. He realized after a week on the job that he wasn't cut out for getting up in the pre-dawn dark to deliver the morning paper, and every day he hit the snooze button. Phone calls started to come in from people on the sister streets complaining that they had nothing to read with their morning coffee. When he asked Josie if she'd take the route off his hands, she jumped around like he had given her a new bike.

In the evenings, she laid all her clothes out on the floor, spreading them out so that they resembled a cartoon character who been steamrolled. When she woke up, she only had to leap into them and run out the door.

In the mornings, a *Toronto Star* van dropped the papers onto her driveway in three large clumps tied in plastic rope. If it was raining or snowing, the piles would come wrapped in clear plastic bags. Josie would pull her wagon from the garage and set to untying and arranging the papers in the order of her route. Tuesdays were coupon days, and it took extra time for her to insert the colourful flyers inside the papers. She would glance at the flyers and take note of the sales at Loblaws, so she could tell her mother later. Her fingers were always stained black from the ink. Since she had a habit of rubbing her face to keep herself awake, Josie would come home from the deliveries and see in the mirror that her cheeks were often smudged black too.

Josie loved her routine and the sense of purpose her job gave her. She loved collecting the money at the end of the week from the neighbours, who often slipped her cookies, candy or even a tip. She saved up her earnings to buy a pair of North Star sneakers that June coveted. A couple of times, June had even come out to help, and there was some talk of expanding the route and splitting the money, but Josie knew it was only a matter of time before June would wuss out. June was more the brains of the pair, and Josie the machine. While June was quick with the numbers—like the papers they needed for the south side of Maud, or the change to give back from five bucks when the total owed was $2.25— June was also a whiner. She would whine about how heavy the papers were to carry, how cold her feet were in the winter, how sleepy she was from waking up so early. Finally, Josie told her she was a one-woman show, and to the relief of them both, June never came out to help again.

Although they were best friends, Josie was often irritated with June. June's parents were fancy, with their Ford station wagon and clothes they took to the dry cleaners. It seemed they had an outfit for every occasion: work clothes, after-work clothes, Sunday clothes, yardwork clothes. June showed Josie her mother's shoe closet once, and Josie marvelled at the sheer number of pairs, and that they were organized according to heel height. Still, June complained about her parents, saying how they were never home and only cared about their jobs. Josie thought at least they had extra money for things like going to the car wash and good after-school snacks.

Josie's parents worked just as much, but they worked with their hands and probably earned half of what June's parents did. Her dad was a mechanic, and her mom worked in a hospital, where she spent all day putting sheets into washers and taking them out to fold. She wore sensible shoes with thick rubber soles, and even with arch supports, her feet ached constantly. Most nights after her mother came home, she made Josie rub her insteps. Josie hated her mother's feet, which were callused and rough, like how Josie's hands were getting.

Josie felt that everything came too easy to June, and June didn't appreciate it. The teachers and even their friends made a fuss about how pretty June was with her dead-straight, shiny hair and tiny-ness, like a China doll, the white neighbours always said. June always got straight As on her report card although she was lazy about studying. And the worst for Josie was that everybody was always going on about how *sweet* June was. Even though Josie was the one who never complained and sucked it up all the time, she would never be the one who got called sweet. Not when her mother made her wash the toilet bowl with a toothbrush or get dinner ready for the whole family when she was working late. Things were expected from her. If she didn't do what she was told, Josie would get whacked with the side of a knife across her bum and scolded that this was the way life was.

So, of course, it figured that June was the one who got a boyfriend first. Josie had always had an eye out for Bruce Wong, her brother's best friend. But Bruce treated Josie like a kid sister, shoving her out of the way as he walked by or cussing her out if she missed a football pass. While Josie gave it right back to him, there was a tiny part of her that wished he was nicer, maybe bringing her a McDonald's milkshake once in a while like he did for June. But what was hardest once he and June started going together was how different Bruce and June acted, like they had secret new personalities. Bruce wore a stupid grin around June, while June became a giggly airhead around Bruce. Josie decided it was best to avoid being around them when they were together. Otherwise, she might have said something mean about them looking dopey, and June would have gotten mad and sad like she did whenever Josie wasn't over-the-top nice to her.

Even with all of this, though, Josie loved June. June

was fiercely loyal. There was that time when Josie found out Mr. Papadakis was beating up his wife. From her bedroom window, she could see into the living room of the Papadakises' house across the street. She'd been woken up by their angry voices shouting on many nights, and she told June about how when she looked out, she'd often see Mr. Papadakis hitting Mrs. Papadakis or gesturing like he might. She figured if he was hitting her in the living room in the middle of the night, he was probably hitting her in other rooms at other times too. The beatings weren't long, a few minutes. She could hear Mr. Papadakis's voice but never Mrs. Papadakis, and Josie sometimes imagined that she was dead. When she told June about it, June had snuck out of her house that same night and stood vigil at Josie's bedroom window, like Wonder Woman. June kept asking Josie if she was okay, sensing how distraught she was even though Josie never said so. They had discussed whether they should tell any of the adults, but when it came down to it, who could they tell? The suicides had rocked their already shaky faith that their parents would know what to do. They knew or were learning fast that the adults were as clueless as the kids. They only had each other.

From then on, June insisted that they let Stephanie Papadakis hang out with them even though Stephanie was annoying because she was always trying too hard to be friends with everybody and sucked at sports. Josie had tried to protest—she didn't see why they had to treat the girl differently because her parents had problems—but June was stubborn about it.

Even though June was a bit of a lazy bum and useless at most things because her parents never made her do any chores, she tried to help Josie do the mountain of housework her mother made her do. On spaghetti nights, June would come over, put on Tim's swim goggles and mince onions for the sauce. She cut herself plenty of times, and Josie had to be the one who sorted through the bloodied bits while June used up all manner of their Band-Aids in the bathroom, but Josie could never get mad at June's sorry, pinched-up face. The girl tried.

But Josie could see the difference in them: June helped out at Josie's house because it was fun to be useful and do the tasks. June didn't have brothers and sisters, and her parents had money to spend on her, and had a cleaning lady come every Friday so their house always smelled like a department store. They didn't want her to babysit or walk dogs because they said studying was the most important thing for her to spend her time on.

For Josie, work was both freedom and a prison. Yet whenever the offer to take on even more work came around, Josie jumped at the chance, considering the money. June would shrug in exasperation. "What's going on, Jos? You planning on making a million by the time you turn fifteen?"

When Josie's young, beautiful aunt Louisa, her father's little sister, got sick with cancer and was undergoing treatment, she and Uncle Bill needed someone to help them around the house. It was the summer, and Josie's father suggested she take the job of being their helper. For some housekeeping and cooking on the weekdays, Aunt Louisa and Uncle Bill gave Josie ten dollars a week. This was easy money as far as Josie was concerned. She adored her aunt and uncle. Josie quit the paper route and devoted herself to her new gig.

Aunt Louisa had a long trail of silken hair that was now falling out by the handful. She was always nice to Josie, offering to teach her how to paint in watercolour and playing her Chinese harp for her. When her aunt performed on her harp, it reminded Josie of falling rain. She was mesmerized by her aunt's long, elegant fingers feathering over the strings to produce the music that always made her feel somehow more Chinese, like a direct connection to her real self. Aunt Louisa remained cheerful even though she could have as easily been snappish or afraid. But that's who she was; everything about her was soft. She made the air seem lighter when she walked into a room. Josie didn't know how she did that, but Aunt Louisa had that effect.

Uncle Bill was a quiet man, but unlike her father, whose quiet was full of weariness. Her uncle's kind of quiet was calm, like the soft-rock music that played in the grocery store that made you want to buy more food. He had slicked-back hair and was always wearing a tie and dress shirt and aviator sunglasses outside. He was also tall and slender and looked a bit like the movie stars in June's mother's Hong

Kong gossip magazines. Josie thought Louisa and Bill were the best-looking adult couple she knew.

It was clear how much Uncle Bill adored Louisa by the way he held her hand when they went for walks around the neighbourhood on Louisa's good days, or by the gentle voice he used when he asked her if she was hungry. Josie had never seen a man take care of a woman before. Although her mother worked the same long hours as her father, it was still up to Josie, her mother and her sister to do all the cooking and cleaning.

Aunt Louisa and Uncle Bill lived a fifteen-minute walk away, outside the enclave of the sister streets. Instead of hanging out with June and the other kids on Winifred after lunch in the August heat, Josie would head over to her aunt and uncle's house to start dinner. When school began that fall, she didn't even wait to walk home with June and dashed to their place right after the bell.

Even though her aunt was sick, they had a lot of fun together. Aunt Louisa would keep her company from a chair in the corner of the kitchen while Josie chopped vegetables or swept. Aunt Louisa, already thin, would sit with her feet on another chair, propped up with pillows and wearing a big scarf around her head. She looked to Josie like a fragile egg, her skin so pale it was almost translucent. Despite the rapid changes to her appearance, Aunt Louisa still liked to talk and asked her about school and her friends in a way her mother never did.

Around late summer, when June was complaining about whether things were working out with Bruce, and Josie was ready to slap her, her aunt took her to the sofa. "What's wrong, Josie? You don't look happy," she said softly. Josie didn't want to burden her aunt, but in a second, she started pouring out her frustrations with June. "June bugs me. She's so whiny. She whines about the stupidest things. Like it rained today, and our hair got wet walking to Mac's. She whined about the rain, but really, what is that going to do? We can't make it stop raining. But she'll go on and on about it, like she's the only one getting wet. And she's so conceited. She picked a rainy day of all days to curl her hair with the curling iron so she could feather it, and she went on about how it took her an hour. Like, who spends an hour on hair?" She realized she was filling the air with stupid things, but it felt great to let the words out.

Aunt Louisa laughed. "Whiny people are the worst!" she said. Josie laughed with her, relieved and surprised that Aunt Louisa wasn't telling her that she was a mean person to be complaining about June, or that she should be a better friend. Josie wondered if this was what it felt like to be an only child.

In the evenings, when Uncle Bill returned home from work, the three of them would have dinner together. Aunt Louisa couldn't eat much, but she and Uncle Bill both always made a fuss about how good the food was that Josie had prepared. It became a ritual that Uncle Bill would take the first bite and chew the food slowly before offering a big thumbs-up. It made Josie want to work even harder for them.

Sometimes when Aunt Louisa was not in the room, Uncle Bill would take Josie's hand in one of his and caress her cheek with the other. The first time he did it was in late September. They were finishing dinner, and Aunt Louisa said she was tired and went upstairs to lie down. He reached over the table and held Josie's hand. At first, she was surprised, taken aback, but then she melted into the warmth of his hand. No one ever touched her this way. Not her mother, not her father. She wondered if this was what other families did, people who loved each other. She looked at Uncle Bill's face and was startled to see the look in his eyes. They seemed glassy, far away. She wondered if it was sadness. He gripped her hand and murmured, "You are so pretty, Josie." Then, as if he was reminded of something, he let go and told her she should go.

That night, as she walked along Samuel Street, the full moon bathed every shadow in white light. It was windy, and the autumn leaves were swirling around on the street. She had a strange stirring in her stomach that matched the churn of leaves. Uncle Bill was from a big family; maybe this was how they expressed themselves when he was growing up. She tried to shrug off the strange feelings. One thing she was sure about was that she was precious to her aunt and uncle, something she had never felt she'd been to anyone. She held on to this and hummed "Weekend in New England" to herself as she went.

Josie started spending more time at their house and hardly saw June. On the Saturday after the hand-holding incident, June cornered her as she was on her way to make their dinner. "Are you going over there again? I thought it was only on school nights, but now weekends too?"

"They need my help. You wouldn't understand these things." Josie meant to hurt June. She knew June would come with her if she invited her, but the last thing she wanted was for her aunt and uncle to meet June and realize that maybe Josie wasn't so pretty or smart or anything after all.

A unt Louisa did not get better with the treatments. By October, she was mostly too weak to get out of bed and couldn't keep Josie company anymore while she did the cleaning and cooking. At dinner, it was only Uncle Bill and Josie at the kitchen table. Uncle Bill still did the thumbs-up, which was sweet, but it felt different without Aunt Louisa's laughter.

Then Aunt Louisa went to hospital and stayed for two weeks. Josie still went over and did the chores, except there was hardly anything to clean because now the house seemed like no one lived there. Uncle Bill was mostly going to the hospital after work, but Josie still cooked dinner and left it on the stove for him. She spent the days feeling like the ground could open up at any time, bracing herself for the worst thing ever to happen.

One night, while she was making congee, Uncle Bill threw open the door, beaming. "She's coming home!" he called out. He paused in the doorway and then strode into the kitchen. Josie turned from her stirring to celebrate with him. He dropped his briefcase and grabbed her up in a bear hug, then kissed her on the lips. Instinctively, she closed her eyes for a second, then opened them wide. He wasn't supposed to be doing this. He was kissing her. His tongue peeped out through his lips and she felt him lick her mouth. His wool coat scratched against her arms and he had stale coffee on his breath. She was staring into his face, an inch from hers, unable to move. He broke the kiss but kept holding her. He pressed her face to his itchy shoulder. "I love you a lot, Josie. You know how much I love you, right?"

Josie nodded against him, bewildered. She loved him too, she thought. He was probably just so excited that Auntie Louisa would be coming home. Maybe he forgot who he was kissing because he was thinking about her aunt. She did something like that once; she'd been talking to her aunt on the phone and then right away had a call with June. When they went to say goodbye, without thinking she said, "I love you." She was mortified, but June didn't even notice, so she let it go. Her aunt had that effect on people.

He kissed her again on her forehead and let her go. "Get home, Josie. I'll take care of the rest of this dinner."

She went to the hallway and quickly pulled on her boots. She grabbed her coat out of the hall closet and shouted, "Okay, bye!" leaving before she'd put it on.

Josie ran all the way home, her coat fluttering behind her in her fist. She dashed into her room and closed her door as quietly as she could. Shaking, she put on her pyjamas and got under the covers. She touched her fingers to her lips. The kiss didn't count. It didn't count. Her thoughts ran in circles. Was it a real kiss? He was her uncle. He wasn't supposed to use his tongue. She felt sick, not in a way she had ever felt sick before. It creeped in from outside of her, seeping in like a cold fog. She felt something bad trying to swallow her. Was Uncle Bill in love with her? Did she do something to make this happen? Was she betraying Aunt Louisa? She curled into a ball and waited for the feeling to pass. Suddenly, she needed June more than she ever had, but she knew she couldn't tell her. June might think it was her fault, something Josie wondered too. She felt very alone.

For the next two days, Josie pretended to have a fever and did such a good job, she got to stay home from school. The first afternoon, June came to visit and sat on the edge of her bed. "What's wrong with you?"

Josie shook her head.

"Is it c-a-n-c-e-r?" It was supposed to be a joke, but Josie started to cry. She rolled over onto her stomach and sobbed into her pillow.

"I'm sorry, Josie. That was such a bad joke. I didn't mean it. You're worried about your aunt. That's why you're sick, and here I am making jokes. I am so sorry."

Josie could feel June's hand rubbing her on the back as if she were a baby. June sounded like she was close to tears too.

Josie sat up and pulled June close to her, and they both cried. It wasn't a baby cry like they did when they got in a fight over nothing. Josie felt it was the kind of cry that came out of a mountain of other held-in cries. There was no relief in her tears or in being in June's arms. She wondered if June could feel the uselessness in it too.

On the third day, Josie's father said Louisa had come home and all of them were going over for dinner that night, so she should cook enough for everyone. She dreaded going, but she was so happy to know her aunt was coming home.

When she arrived, Uncle Bill was in the kitchen, making tea. "Hello, Miss Josie. Go on up and see your aunt Louisa!" He seemed so normal, as if nothing had happened. Josie was relieved and rushed upstairs to see her aunt, taking the stairs two at a time. Maybe nothing *had* happened, and it was in her imagination. When she opened the door to the bedroom, she wasn't prepared for what she saw. Aunt Louisa was even thinner than she'd remembered. Her face, once so full, like a ripe peach, as her father used to say, had become sunken, as if the peach had been plucked and only the memory of it remained. She didn't have one of her beautiful floral scarves on, and her head was now completely free of hair. Deep purple smudged her eyes, as if she had been beaten up. When Josie found the courage to enter, Aunt Louisa couldn't even speak. She only lifted her left hand slightly to greet her.

Her parents came later, and they visited with Aunt Louisa for only five minutes before leaving her to rest. Josie had cooked lasagna like her mother had taught her. Uncle Bill didn't give her the thumbs-up and her mother complained the noodles were overcooked. Josie couldn't even taste it. There was very little conversation and some mention about "keeping her comfortable." Then her parents got up to leave and told Josie to please stay back and help clean up before heading home. Uncle Bill needed the help.

Josie started to feel dread like rocks gathering in her stomach and filling up to her chest. From the other room, she heard the door close after her parents and uncle said their goodbyes. She busily gathered the dishes and filled the sink with warm water and soap. She didn't hear him coming because the water was on full blast, she didn't want to hear him coming, but she was surprised when she felt his embrace from behind. He wrapped his arms around her and pressed his body into her back. She felt very small. She didn't know what to do; she was frozen inside but her limbs still moved, so she turned off the faucet and started to wash the dishes. She felt his mouth on her neck, his tongue leaving a trail of wet saliva. Josie was in shock, her body a lit ember.

Josie scrubbed a spot on a bowl while he pressed himself harder into her back. She felt Uncle Bill's penis, hard and fat, rubbing on her bum while he buried his face in her hair. Did she wash her hair that day? She couldn't remember. Her mother often asked to sniff her head to determine if she had bathed. "You stink like cat piss. What kind of girl are you? No one will want to marry a girl with a head that smells like cat piss."

She finished that bowl and another and started on the lasagna pan, scrubbing for her life. He let her go, and she paused in the aftermath, the sudden cold air against her back. She picked up the scouring pad.

"Lock up on your way out, Josie." He leaned over and planted a kiss on the top of her head. "You're such a special girl." His steps faded as he walked out of the kitchen, down the hall and up the stairs.

On the walk to school the next day, June was whining about Bruce not coming around anymore. "I guess he's done with me. Do you think that's it? Did he say anything to you? Or to your brother?"

"My aunt Louisa is dying." No one had said it yet, but Josie knew.

"Oh my God, Josie." That was all June said. Then she

took Josie's hand, and they walked to school holding hands like they used to. Josie was grateful that June always knew what to do in moments like these. Her hand in June's warm one made her believe that things could still turn around.

Josie wanted to tell June about Uncle Bill, but she didn't know what to tell. That her uncle loved her too much? She wasn't even sure how to describe what had happened. She had felt special to her aunt and uncle. She knew she *was* special to them. Maybe that specialness was something indescribable, and her uncle was acting a bit crazy because his wife was dying. Josie turned it over in her head many times, searching for answers. Maybe it wasn't even wrong what happened. There was no harm done, right? There were no bruises or scars like what happened to Mrs. Papadakis. But still, these were the kinds of questions she wanted to ask June, but that she knew June wouldn't know how to answer.

Eight days later, Aunt Louisa died. During those days, there wasn't even the chance to talk or say goodbye because a nurse started coming around twice daily to inject her with morphine. This sent her aunt to another place, and even when she appeared awake, she wasn't. Nothing further happened with Uncle Bill in those eight days when Josie continued to go and make him dinner. He still paid her on the Friday, as he always did. He didn't go to work all that week and made a point of thanking her for every meal, even though it didn't seem like he ate anything the whole time. Each day, Josie found the food still on the stove from the night before.

When Aunt Louisa did die, in the middle of the night, Uncle Bill told everybody that it was peaceful. Josie didn't know what that meant or looked like, but she guessed her aunt was blissed out on morphine and slipped away. The funeral followed shortly after, and Josie was upset it was an open casket. Her aunt did not look anything like she did in real life, before the c-a-n-c-e-r took away her beauty. The makeup artist put a lot of foundation on her, and she looked like she had an orange tan. Her aunt's lips were painted a dark cranberry. This made Josie angry. Aunt Louisa never wore makeup because she never had to. Her lips were naturally a shade of pink that had always reminded Josie of the crabapple blossoms in spring. They had tied one of her scarves around her head the way she did after losing her hair. It was the scarf with butterflies and daisies. At least they had chosen well for that.

Josie did not cry at the funeral. Her father bawled like a baby, something she had never seen before. Her mom had to put her arms around his waist to steady him as he walked down the chapel aisle to leave. This was something else she didn't think she had ever seen before—her mother touching her father. June had wanted to come, but she called that morning to say her parents wouldn't let her. June had never been to a funeral before. Josie wondered what they were worried about.

After Aunt Louisa died, Josie's parents nudged her to keep going to help out Uncle Bill. He wouldn't eat unless she made him dinner, they said. Josie tried to explain that her schoolwork had gotten especially heavy and she needed to study more. Her mom called her a brat for being so selfish at a time like this, when Aunt Louisa and Uncle Bill had treated her so well and needed her more than ever.

Josie was a worker. She was not a brat. She went back to the cooking and cleaning for Uncle Bill. She had the key and would race there the minute school was out so she could make the food, tidy and leave before Uncle Bill got home from work, but he started coming home earlier than he ever had. Uncle Bill was not himself; he was not who he had always been. He would come to her swiftly while she was doing whatever she was doing, grab her and hold her to him, sometimes kissing her on the mouth and pushing his tongue in, and once, he started making little panting noises and wrestled up her T-shirt to feel her mosquito-bite-sized breasts. Each time, he was becoming wilder. He ground his torso against her back and breathed heavily into her hair. And then he would stop, not because she wrenched away but because he wrenched himself away. Every time, he would turn around and jam his hand into the air in front of him like he was stopping a runaway subway train. "I love you so much, Josie. You are very special to me, to us." He started doubling her pay, giving her twenty bucks each week.

∞∞∞

One morning before school, June came by the house as usual to pick her up. June stared at Josie, who'd taken to holding her books against her chest and walking with her head thrust forward like a turtle.

"That's it," June said, yanking on Josie's upper arm and pulling her in the opposite direction.

"What are you doing, June? Quit fooling around. We're going to be late."

"You and me are ditching school, Jos." June's grip was fierce. Josie was perplexed; between the two of them, June was definitely the rule abider.

"Where are we going?"

"Ditching school. The mall. We're going to walk around, eat lunch in the food court, and then I'm going to take you to a matinee." She poked Josie in the shoulder. "You. Need. Cheering. Up." She grinned. "Besides, I need to get my mind off my love life." For a moment, Josie's mood picked up. Playing hooky and going to the mall was a pretty big no-no. Their parents would ground them for a lifetime. They were only allowed to go to the mall on Saturdays, and even then, June's parents didn't always grant her that. This was an adventure, and she and June hadn't had one in a long time.

For the first time since the whole Bruce thing started, Josie had never been happier to hear her friend complain. They cowered in the back corner of the bus shelter, waiting for the Warden bus, their backs to the street in case a passing car contained a parent who would tell on them. Finally, the bus came, they got seats, and the landscape went by, squat strip malls in shades of grey. Josie sat without speaking, gazing through the filthy glass even though June tried to talk to her.

"So, what film do you want to see, huh? *Amityville Horror* is playing still. You wanted to see that?" June hated scary movies but knew Josie loved them. Josie pressed the back of June's hand with hers and nodded, still staring out the window. June also fell silent.

The stores weren't even open yet when they arrived. They strolled through the empty mall, looking in the store windows to kill time. Empty of people except for some custodians pushing large mops, the place felt eerie

"Hey, Jos. Can you talk to me? Like, tell me about your aunt if you want. Anything."

They were stopped in front of Fairweather, and the Christmas display was already up. The lady mannequins stared at them with vacant eyes among reindeer and tinsel. June and Josie were dressed in the outfits that they'd bought together here, at this mall: matching coats, but June's was red where hers was navy, same Cougar boots, same hats with different coloured stripes and pompoms. They could have been twins. The details of their faces were lost in the reflection but Josie knew June was staring at her.

She opened her palm for June to take. June grabbed on to it instantly and squeezed. Josie took a breath and considered, measured and weighed her heart against June's tender one. Because Josie knew June as well as she knew herself, she knew what her best friend could and could not bear.

"You're right, June. I really miss my aunt," Josie said as June leaned her head against Josie's shoulder.

Things

Darren's mother sucked her teeth, in the Jamaican way. This, Darren knew, meant trouble. He stared at the red-inked "6/10" on the math test in his hand. A pass was still good, but his mother did not think it was good enough. He knew from the teeth-sucking and the long pause that followed that a lecture was coming.

"Boy, what did I tell you? You have to do better than that. I didn't come to this country and scrub all those toilets so that my own can't pass a math test, you hear?" Her voice always got louder, and her patois stronger, as she got madder.

"But I did pass!" he shouted. He knew instantly that this was the wrong, wrong move. Her pause this time deepened and changed position; he saw the storm gather in her eyes. And then, *whack*. Right across his cheek. It smarted, but he blinked and held himself together.

She pointed to the stairs, too angry to say more. He thumped up to his room to show her that he was mad too.

127

He didn't know the exact target of his anger, but it didn't matter. He was mad.

Darren stayed in his room and read comic books, trying to ignore the rumblings in his stomach. After it was seven, he guessed that there would be no dinner. He tried to concentrate on the Fantastic Four, but his head kept going back to the math test. He had told his mother that he was studying that night, but he'd spent the time drawing comics instead. Darren felt a bit of guilt about that, but just a bit. He had spent the night drawing a supervillain named Galactus to match the Thing, his favourite of the Fantastic Four. The Thing was really a guy named Ben Grimm. He got exposed to radiation, and as a result, his skin became covered with large plates of craggy rocks and boulders. He was orangey brown—not an easy colour to create with his pencil crayons—but Darren mixed No. 2 Sarasota Orange and No. 11 Chestnut Brown and got something pretty close. His mother wouldn't buy him the twenty-four pack of Laurentian pencil crayons because she said twelve was enough. Nav had the pack of twenty-four because his family was rich from owning Mac's Milk. If Darren had had the twenty-four, he would have mixed Sarasota Orange with No. 21 Indian Red, and it would have looked perfect.

The Thing might have been known as the monster of the Fantastic Four, but Darren thought he was the smartest. He and Danny, the resident comics expert over at Mac's, debated this point a lot. Danny thought the Human Torch was smarter and that fire was stronger than brute strength. Darren agreed that while those things were true, the Torch could only hold his fire body for seventeen hours before burning out, so that was pretty limited. Nav thought Sue Reed, also known as the Invisible Woman, was the be all and end all. She may have been pretty and blond, but Darren thought invisibility could only do so much. Since Nav was Darren's best friend, when Nav said his favourite was the Invisible Woman with that dopey smile on his face, Darren had to let him be happy and think whatever he wanted.

Most importantly, the Thing, with his tough skin that could withstand bullets and bombs, was constantly jumping in front of danger to shield his friends and innocent bystanders. It wasn't that the Thing was indestructible— his rock surface could be penetrated by extremely lethal weaponry—but the Thing always took the chance and never backed down. And the Thing was funny. He was the only one of the Fantastic Four with any sense of humour, and boy did he make Darren laugh. Being funny was its own special power.

Darren and Nav had decided that they would create their first comic book together. Even though Nav had the better art supplies, he was more of a word man, and it was decided that Darren would be in charge of the drawing while Nav would write the story. The project became their obsession, the object on which all their thoughts focused.

Still trapped in his room at seven-thirty, Darren, trying

not to think about how hungry he was, was drawing flying caterpillars dropping all over the Thing when his door creaked open. He didn't look up, not wanting to give his mother the satisfaction. She placed a tray on his desk, beside his sketchbook, and said, "Eat your vegetables."

He waited until she shut the door to look down at the tray. Rice, chicken and corn. He grinned and shut his book.

The year before, he had announced to his mother that when he grew up, he was going to be a comic book artist. He always got good marks in art. She was not impressed until he reasoned that when he got famous, he would make enough money to take care of them both. Maybe they could move to Florida and swim in the sea every day. He drew this picture with Nav's No. 13 Ultramarine Blue for the sea and figures of him and his mother standing in it. He considered his No. 12 Black to draw them, but he wasn't black. Neither was his mother. They were both No. 10 Photo Brown. He was a bit Chestnut Brown too, but his mother was also No. 26 Burnt Sienna, a colour that even Nav didn't have. Only the luckiest kids could afford the thirty-six-pack Laurentians.

"Oh, I like the sea!" his mother had said.

On most days, she looked at his drawings and smiled big. On those good days, they would turn up their stereo and dance in the living room. The sound of Peter Tosh or Aretha Franklin filled the house. On weekends if his mother wasn't working a shift at the hospital, her friends would come over, and Darren would take turns dancing with the aunties.

Other days, she told him not to waste his time; there were no Black superheroes. Darren told her that was only partially true. Danny had said there was Luke Cage, Hero for Hire, but those comics never made it to Mac's Milk. And the Thing may have been orange, but Darren knew in his heart that he was actually Black.

Darren also did pretty well in science. He loved bringing home good marks. His mother would take the As, pin them on the corkboard and say, "Keep your head down and do your work. Don't make a fuss. Don't look them in the eye. Get the good marks, get the graduation paper and get out. That's all that matters."

She talked to him like he were a train already in full motion and she wanted him to stay that way. "You remember that, Darren. That's how you'll get by in this country." Other kids got bedtime stories; he got lectures on how to get by. She'd be rubbing lotion into her hands, which were always cracked because she had to wash them so much, shaking her head like something had reminded her of something else.

"But what if they ask me to look at them?" He'd try not to sound exasperated, but he was. He'd bring home an A, and she'd tell him not to look at people. The lines in the conversation didn't even cross a little.

Her brown eyes would bore holes into him like Cyclops, who shot laser beams from his eye visor. "Son, they never will."

There were things that his mother said that he didn't understand, and things he didn't feel she understood about

131

him. For instance, Darren was pretty sure he had secret powers like the superheroes in his comics. The time in Grade 6 when he beat up Larry Lems confirmed this suspicion. It was during lunch one day, and he, Nav, June and Josie were eating their bag lunches on the field. It was the first warm day in spring, and the ground was dry with brown patches of grass and dirt. Larry Lems approached them and said he was hungry. If Larry had been a nice person, Darren would have shared his baloney sandwich, but this was Larry Lems, and he didn't ask nicely. Darren said, "Get lost, Larry. Not our problem that your dad doesn't feed you." Maybe that was harsh, but Larry was always trying to start something with the other kids.

This set Larry off. His face got really red (like No. 3 Poppy Red) and he yelled, "Don't talk to me like that, nigger. Don't even look at me. Your mom's a dirty nigger. I wouldn't eat the sandwich she touched."

Before even thinking, Darren got up and was on Larry. Larry was a good fifteen pounds heavier and three inches taller, but a supernatural strength had taken control of Darren's body. He felt no fear, just the power in his arms, as he punched Larry again and again until Larry's nose squirted blood as red as his face and it spilled onto the ground. Some kid ran and got a teacher from inside the school, and Darren felt large hands try to pull him off Larry. Even the teacher struggled because Darren was still possessed by the otherworldly strength.

While it made him a hero among the kids at school, he got a detention and a call to his mother from the principal. That night, she gave him a whooping on his bum. She didn't want to hear an explanation. He had bitten back the tears while his mother cried as she hit him. After she was spent, she grabbed on to him and hugged him hard. This was when he understood that his strong mother was sometimes afraid, and this frightened him in turn.

He didn't think she needed to be afraid. Darren liked school and his friends and making everyone laugh in class. It was his particular talent, like the Thing. And his teachers for the most part thought he was hilarious. They told his mother in teacher-parent interviews, "Darren is a really funny kid!" and his mother would politely say thank you. Only afterward, in the car, would she smack him in the head, suck her teeth and tell him that "funny" was not what education was for.

"But we laugh all the time at home!" he would protest.

"You will always get your laughs at home, son. But at school, you work!"

Then in Grade 7 he got a new teacher, a little man with bright yellow hair and a moustache who wore plaid suits. Mr. Wilson had a face that didn't quite match Laurentian No. 14, the pencil crayon called Flesh. Darren and Nav had once had a long discussion about who did actually have skin that matched No. 14 and could only settle on one kid in the class, Tracy McTavish. Her flesh was what Laurentian had modelled the colour after, they decided. The rest of them had skin that you had to blend two or three colours together to get. Nav's skin also had a base of No. 10 Photo Brown but shaded lightly with the pencil and with an even lighter touch of No. 1 Deep Yellow applied on top.

Mr. Wilson was something like a No. 18 Blush Pink with a hint of No. 19 Cherry Red around the cheeks. He was strict in some ways and gave a lot of homework, but he also had a fun side that he showed through the stories he'd tell at the end of every day. He always talked about how in his hometown of Cobourg, a little town by a lake, he and his best friend, Peter, would have all kinds of adventures and get into buckets of trouble. One time, they put earthworms inside girls' sandwiches, and in the middle of the night one year, they took screwdrivers to their school sign, so that in the morning the sign said "lover Lane Public School" instead of "Clover Lane Public School." Darren thought Mr. Wilson was wicked smart and a significant improvement over their previous teacher, whose personality was like a used-up tea bag.

The problem was Mr. Wilson didn't take to Darren the way Darren had hoped. When Darren tried to crack a joke, thinking he and his teacher were on the same team, Mr. Wilson called him a distraction. The kids had always laughed when Darren did something funny in class, but after a few of these episodes, they became too scared to react. Once, Mr. Wilson got so annoyed, he put Darren in the far corner of the room and taped his legs to the chair.

Mr. Wilson didn't treat the other kids this harshly. Darren knew that he was not the best student in the class, but he didn't deserve what Mr. Wilson dished out. He seemed to like the white kids just fine. Even with Damian, the dumbest one around, Mr. Wilson had absolute patience. While the other students exchanged eye rolls as Damian struggled over a simple multiplication problem on the blackboard, Mr. Wilson explained in an encouraging voice for the millionth time about moving decimals. With the other kids who weren't white, like June and Nav, Mr. Wilson expected great things, which wasn't hard since June and Nav almost always got good grades. The occasional time that June passed notes or was caught whispering to Josie, Mr. Wilson only expressed disappointment by sighing and saying, "June, are you finished with your social engagements and ready to join us again?" But for Darren, there was no slack. He tried to stay quiet, do his work, but no matter what, Mr. Wilson found something that wasn't right. He even chewed Darren out for forgetting to take his baseball cap off and said Darren lacked respect.

There was another black student in the class, Tanya, whom his mother would have described as big-boned. She hardly ever spoke, though, and most people didn't notice her. Mr. Wilson acted like she wasn't even there. She sat in the corner, with tight braids, and big glasses taking over her face, silent and expressionless. But once in a while, Darren saw that as she listened to the lesson or was engrossed in a book, her eyes were alive. Darren thought Tanya had a strange ability. She was so visible and yet invisible. But perhaps the ability wasn't in her but in others. They chose to look or they didn't.

Darren didn't tell his mother about how Mr. Wilson treated him, not even about the leg-taping incident, because she would get angry and say he'd brought it upon himself. She might even do what she'd been threatening to do with him for years and send him back to Jamaica. It was her home, but he'd never been there and couldn't tell whether she loved or hated it. Almost every day, his mother told him the same thing: he had to try harder and be better than everyone else or he would be sent back home, where there was nothing for him—no school, no money, no life. Darren knew Jamaica had its problems, but he also knew it had palm trees and coconuts and the ocean and a father—things he had never seen before and wanted to. So, in the end, maybe going there wouldn't be so bad.

His father occasionally appeared through letters with loopy handwriting. There would be a quick note at the bottom of letters to his mother, that read: "Dear Son, I am well. Hope you are too. Work hard for your mother. Father." He would ask his mother to cut these sections out, and he would collect the clippings in a shoebox. She would oblige but told him not to get his hopes up. He never told his mother that he imagined his dad to be the Thing. He also thought that this father would welcome him with open arms, and that together they would fight all the mysterious forces that were wrong with Jamaica that Darren's mother only hinted at but never explained.

Darren knew his mother had worked hard to get them this house in this nice neighbourhood and all their nice furniture. She reminded him all the time as if he weren't listening. But Darren was listening. He knew her story well. She came to Canada alone when she was only eighteen. She said she scrubbed enough toilets in other people's homes to put herself through nursing school and finally landed a good job at a hospital as an emergency room nurse. Darren didn't know how many toilets it took to pay for school, and from the time when he was very young, whenever she talked of those years, he imagined an endless row of them stretching to the horizon.

Now, she could hold her head up high because she had a good job and all those white people needed her when they were at their weakest. In the neighbourhood, when the parents were killing themselves, she was the one who met the bodies at the hospital and gently wrapped them in sheets before delivering them to the morgue. When Darren asked her what the dead parents had looked like, she said, "Like used Kleenex." Darren pictured a crumbled-up mess of tissue and shuddered. He thought he would never want to touch a dead person and imagined his mother's matter-of-fact hands getting to work to wash a dead body.

Darren thought about his mother's hands a lot, those

hands that cupped his face when she wanted a kiss, that cared for sick people, that massaged lotion on her legs and that had touched death. Those hands were their own special colour that he couldn't capture with the Laurentian pencil crayons. Darren imagined he would need paint to mix the perfect hue. The palms of her hands were made up of the most beautiful purples, browns, pinks and yellows. He was not afraid of those hands. He was proud of them and welcomed them even when they smacked him in the head when he was disobedient. Darren knew that all the lessons were held in his mother's hands.

Darren was convinced that she had worked too hard to get to where she was and would never kill herself like the others and abandon him. Darren once asked why the parents had done it. Why they had wanted to become like used Kleenex.

"They were sad, and that kind of sadness is the worst kind of sadness," she answered.

"Are we that kind of sad, Mom?"

She laughed for a long time and walked away. Darren still heard her laughing as she walked from the kitchen to the living room. Finally, he heard her voice from the other room: "Does it sound like we're sad?" and more laughter. He knew his mother was not like those fragile parents who threw themselves like snot-filled tissue in the trash can. But he still worried about making her sad, the other particular power he seemed to have that he didn't want. Darren dreaded the day when Mr. Wilson and his mother would meet. Because way worse than her being angry was when she was sad, especially if he was the cause of it. Still, it seemed that in her, anger and sadness came together like rivers running into each other until you couldn't tell them apart.

Darren felt a glimmer of hope during class one day when Mr. Wilson announced that they would take an important math test, and if they did well on it, they might qualify to be in a math competition with another area school. Darren had abandoned all hope that he and his teacher would be friends, but he started to imagine how happy his mother would be if he made the math team. The thought of it made him feel good.

Beginning that night, he did his homework and even went ahead into the next chapter. He also started going over to Nav's house to get help from his smart sister, Archana, who was in Grade 8. Nav's parents took homework very seriously and made Nav and Archana do at least one hour of it every day. Normally, that would just about kill Darren. He thought he did a lot of studying too, but he'd had to make his own barometer for what "a lot" was since his mother was always at work and it was up to him to decide.

But this math competition dangled in front of him. He wanted it. He spent a few afternoons at the Sharmas' dining room table and studied with Nav. He loved going there; their house always smelled of curry—not like his mother's curry, sharper, sweeter. If it weren't for Archana, he might have spent even more time there. Unlike Nav, who was a nice kid, Archana was sour and mean. She had long, straight hair that fell down her back like an arrow, long arms and knobby limbs. Archana was the kind of skinny that would make Darren's mother suck her teeth and want to fatten her up with some goat stew. But what she lacked in fat, Archana made up in mean. Every one of those afternoons he was over to study, she would pace behind him and Nav with a wooden yardstick as they worked at the problems she made up.

"No talking. Don't even look at each other!" Her voice was so serious and pretend grown-up, Nav and Darren couldn't resist giggling.

Whack. She cracked the yardstick on the table between them, and they shut up and went back to their problems. Nav was used to her and would smile at Darren like it was nothing, but Darren wanted to punch her in the teeth. Still, Darren knew that if he was going to get a good mark on the test, he had to do whatever skinny-mean Archana wanted, so he stuck with it.

One afternoon following a cruel session filled with whacks that barely missed his head, he and Nav went upstairs to his room and pored over the comics. Nav was the luckiest guy in the world because his parents got copies of the comics that were delivered to their store. He had stacks and stacks of them beside his bed.

"Do you think we're going to do okay on that test, Nav?" Darren asked while they flipped through the latest X-Men.

"Sure, Darren. You're going to do great." Nav was so shy

he mostly only spoke to Darren, June and Josie. His voice was deep and coarse, not like what you'd expect from a tiny, shy boy who had big Bambi eyes. Nav was too scared to talk to Darren's mother, but she liked him anyway. She said he was too pretty to be a boy but that he was a good influence.

"I hope so. My mom was mad at me after the last test."

Nav smiled at Darren and reached over to pat him on the back. Nav sometimes seemed a lot older to Darren than he was. Only parents and teachers ever patted you like that.

"Wilson is out to get me, Nav. I can feel it."

Darren tried to behave the way he thought his teacher wanted, but lately, even his breathing seemed to bother him. Darren felt like he was on permanent detention. When Mr. Wilson got irritated, he would stroke his moustache with his index finger. Sometimes Mr. Wilson made him clean the blackboard and brushes, but often he told Darren to sit quietly at his desk and do nothing. He said it would teach Darren discipline, which he clearly lacked. Darren wasn't even allowed to read his comics while Mr. Wilson sat at his desk at the front of the room doing his teacher things, only occasionally pausing to look up at him with a cold stare. His mean wasn't like Archana's mean. It had a bright hue, like Hulk's arch-enemy and nemesis the Abomination, No. 8 Emerald Green. Darren would quickly look down, pretending there was something on his nails, finding it easy to take his mother's advice. There was no way he would look into those eyes. He might disintegrate or something.

141

But in those last fifteen minutes of school, no matter what had happened during the day, Mr. Wilson would tell his stories to the class. His face would soften, and Darren watched his teacher perch on the edge of his desk to talk about his childhood adventures with his best friend, Peter. Darren had to admit he loved the stories. As much as he tried to hate his teacher, he couldn't resist being pulled into them. It was hard to hold the two Mr. Wilsons straight, the irritated one and the sentimental one. Maybe being two entirely different people was Mr. Wilson's secret power. Darren believed that everyone had one. And as long as Mr. Wilson didn't call home to complain to his mother, he decided he could deal with whatever was thrown at him.

The day after the math test, Mr. Wilson handed the tests back to the students by calling out their names. When they came up to get their papers, he said things like "Good work, Mary" or "You can do better, James." Nav went up when his name was called, and being Nav, he stared at the ground when Mr. Wilson said, "Excellent, Naveen." Everyone had gone up already, and finally, he called Darren. He got up excitedly, already picturing his mother finally smiling about a math test and putting it on the fridge. Maybe she would even take him to Kentucky Fried Chicken that night for a bucket.

"Darren. Here is your test." He held the paper in front of Darren. Darren looked at it. While there were check marks all over it, acknowledging that the answers were right, at the top it said "0." He didn't understand.

"I will not tolerate cheating," Mr. Wilson said in a low, deadly voice.

Darren kept his eyes on the paper and tried to process his shock. "I didn't cheat." The words burst out of Darren as if he'd been pushed from behind. He almost went to apologize for saying them, but then he stopped himself. He was mad.

"Yes, you did. I am sure you looked at Naveen's paper while you wrote the test. There is no way you could have gotten a perfect score on it." He held the paper just out of reach from Darren, not letting go even as Darren tried to take it.

"I did not!" he shouted. He silently apologized to his mother, but Mr. Wilson was wrong. This was all wrong.

"Did you raise your voice at me?" Mr. Wilson's tone got even lower and nastier. If his words had been written in a comic, they would have had a jagged bubble around them.

"But, Mr. Wilson, I did not cheat, I swear!" Darren had carefully taken his voice down, but he thought it came out whiny.

"That's it. Detention. A week."

Darren looked back at his friends, sitting in rows with blank expressions on their faces. When he tried to catch their eyes, they all looked down at their desks. If he were to draw them, they would be heads with no faces.

A memory flashed into his mind. The day he and his mother were walking through Agincourt Mall, eating ice

cream with candy pieces in it. His mother had been picking out the candy in hers and giving it to him. Then, out
of the blue, she took his hand in hers and made them stop
walking. "When you grow up," she said, "it won't happen slowly, like it does for other kids. It will happen all at
once. On that day, you will change, and you will remember that day, that moment, for the rest of your life." They
continued strolling on the shiny floor, past the arcade and
Birks jewellery.

Darren had a perfect image of that scene in his mind.
The things she told him that he had half-listened to crys-
tallized as he was standing in front of the man who had his
perfect test in his hand. Darren held it all, everything he
knew up to that point.

Darren looked up to meet Mr. Wilson's face, his small
glasses perched on that nose that Darren could draw with
one curved line, that moustache that was so yellow it could've
been twisted onto a plate beside some pancakes. Chalk dust
bit into his nose. Behind him, the class was tomb-silent
except for some kids passing by in the hall, laughing. He
lifted his eyes and locked them on Mr. Wilson's small, hard
eyes, tired brown like dusty marbles.

Something in those eyes startled Darren. It was beyond
the scope of the test, of the classroom, of what stood between
them. There was no trace of kindness, not anything left over
from the boy from Cobourg who had fun with his buddy.
There was hardness, an unrelenting hardness. From the cor-

ner of Darren's eyes, he thought he saw a flash of orange. It was a mix of No. 2 Sarasota Orange and No. 11 Chestnut Brown, to be precise.

Darren took a deep breath and without breaking his stare, he told Mr. Wilson, "No."

Sweets

Her English was not good, but she knew what they were asking. Their three pairs of eyes were on her granddaughter, June, who was turning red like a tomato. Poh Poh smirked and continued to throw handfuls of candy from the plastic bag onto the table. She didn't know what June replied, but it was a long, breathless statement. Poh Poh wasn't bothered. She was used to it.

She wondered what the four children saw. She bet they had never seen the likes of her. She looked at her hands, speckled, fingers crooked as she threw their treasured sweets into the centre of the table. She was old, but she was still strong, and she made a point of tossing the candy hard, so that some of it bounced off the surface and clattered to the linoleum floor. Her hair was white and cut back to the scalp. Her broad, flat back was curved like a crane's. She was dressed in her standard black pants and black sweater. Never makeup. Nails short and square. She felt the children looking her up and down and wondered what parts of her they thought were woman, what parts man? She wondered why it was so important that they always had to know. But she knew they wondered. She knew they cared.

When she first arrived in this country, all Poh Poh wanted to do was lie in her soft bed, eat sweets and feel her body spread large. She liked to let the candy melt slowly until it became a tiny heart on her tongue that she could crack apart with her teeth. She wanted to be left alone to think of nothing in this nothing place where you could walk and walk for hours but never arrive anywhere new. There were the same houses, the same colourless faces of the *gweilos*, the squat supermarkets.

For many years after her husband died, she made money managing the dried goods store in Hong Kong so she could send her daughter overseas for school. The day came when her daughter, Mei, thought it was time that she repaid her poor old mother by bringing her to her adopted country and making her live there for the rest of her days. Poh Poh knew what this was—her last showdown. She had been brought here to be coddled, to be given blank time until she grew completely dependent on her daughter, and then, quietly, she would die. This was the filial duty, and all the neighbours in Hong Kong had been envious of this obedient and loving daughter bringing her to *Gum San*, the promised land where the skies were bluest. She knew her daughter wanted her to have a good death after a life of sweat, hustle and hardness.

Mei expected her mother to go soft in all the right places. She thought her mother would appreciate the tranquility. Sometimes Poh Poh wondered if this daughter of hers ever knew her at all.

Poh Poh bit her sharp tongue because she saw how hard her daughter tried—the pull at the corners of her mouth, her eyes becoming glossy when Poh Poh snapped at her to leave her alone. Poh Poh saw especially her daughter's false cheerfulness. Mei made everything sound like a party. "Ma, isn't this the biggest grocery store you've ever seen? And so clean! Not like the wet markets in Hong Kong. See how everything is so organized? Look at the colour of the corn!" and "Ma, see how wide the roads are here? So much space and never a traffic jam! We don't ever have to be late here! Everyone is always early!" and "Ma, doesn't the washing machine clean so well? The clothes always smell so good, huh? Like lemons! Who thought clothes could smell like fruit?"

Poh Poh had arrived in the winter, which was a cruel joke in and of itself. When she finally donned all the gear Mei had bought for her and went outside by herself to examine this place her daughter thought so highly of, she slipped and fell on a patch of ice, and her daughter chastised her. Her daughter said she could have broken a leg. No more walks, she decreed. Mei fussed and cooed with too much worry, too much talk. Volume turned too high. Poh Poh returned to her room and nursed her bruised knee, wanting to shut Mei's voice out. She watched the afternoon matinees on TV to pass the time. Old westerns. Shoot-'em-ups. She knew them all.

After the first month of Poh Poh lying in her bed, Mei suggested that she knit. Poh Poh sneered. She didn't want to knit. She had never knitted and never would. Mei asked her to teach June how to read and write in Chinese. She was no teacher. Her daughter gave her instructions on how to live, what to wear to the mall (the ugly blue shoes with cheap rubber soles), what apples to buy at Dominion (Never the green ones. Too sour. Pick the ones with little feet on them. They were called *Dee-li-shush* for good reason), how to answer the phone ("Hello? Not home. Call later.") She was her daughter's child now.

Mei wanted her to think everything was perfect, and if only she would let her guide her, her mother would see that too. But Poh Poh didn't think this place was so perfect—grass grew everywhere in summer like a rash, and snow piled high in the winter. These people were servants to the seasons, always turning on sprinklers and lawnmowers, or stooping over to shovel snow or rake leaves. So much wasted energy.

One night in the summer, when they sat in the backyard on hard outdoor chairs, Mei told her that some people had killed themselves on the street two years before she came. Her daughter told her in hushed tones, as death was not something to talk about out loud. It came as no surprise to Poh Poh. People killed themselves and each other all the time in Hong Kong. Did these people think that having perfect grass all over the place would change that kind of anger?

Poh Poh watched her westerns, listened to Cantonese opera, read the Hong Kong gossip magazines that her daughter bought in Chinatown when they were already a month old. She made rice and side dishes while her daughter and her husband were at work, and napped until the household came home for dinner.

In the afternoons, June and her friends came home from school and broke the quiet like a window. At the same time every day, Poh Poh could hear the four storm in. They threw their piles of coats and bags on the floor. Their shoes and boots left puddles and streaks of mud. Their lunch boxes smelled sour. They would always follow June to the fridge for milk and snacks. When it was nice outside, they would return to the street and play in a noisy riot with the other children. When it was raining or too cold, they huddled around the television in the living room, and their voices and laughter drifted to Poh Poh's room upstairs. She would grumble to herself that her granddaughter was a disrespectful wretch.

At the beginning, Poh Poh did not have much to say to this foreign granddaughter. Poh Poh disliked her. June spoke in another language entirely that was not Cantonese and no English she'd ever heard. The girl demanded to eat dinner in front of the TV. She giggled when things were not funny. She spoke back to her parents, and they did nothing but shake their heads. Poh Poh had told Mei that if it were up to her, she would smack June with an open hand if she disrespected her in such a way, but Mei was horrified. "Things are different here, Ma," she said, before fleeing the room. Poh Poh was old enough to know her daughter was wrong. Things and people didn't change. This place may have been bland as a bowl of plain rice, but in essence, in its operation, it was like any other, and so were the people.

Poh Poh, not wanting to attempt the sidewalks again during the winter, had become a squirrel, collecting bags of chocolate bars and hard candies throughout the warm months, hoarding enough of them to last her through that next winter. Each afternoon, alone in her room, she would take out her false teeth, close her eyes, and suck the sweets slowly. This smallest pleasure was enough to get her through the day.

Poh Poh couldn't figure out how June knew she had the stash or where to find it, but she did and managed to ruin all of Poh Poh's hard work in one afternoon. Poh Poh had woken to hear June rifling through her things, but she kept her back turned to the wall and pretended to be asleep. She heard June click the closet door closed, tiptoe out and then run down the stairs with her elephant feet. Then Poh Poh heard the muffled snickering in the kitchen and the sickening thump of all the sweets being dumped on the table. She was furious. If only she could have slapped June and berated her in front of her friends. That would have taught her a lesson about stealing.

But today, she was in the kitchen, ready for them. As they entered, she reached into her bag of supplies and threw the candy on the table dramatically. A rainbow of wrappers and foil sprayed across the scratched surface and bounced onto the floor. There was a moment of shock as the children registered what was happening. Then they erupted in cheers and applause. June kept her eyes down and turned red. It was a reaction she had often, and it grated on her grandmother. She wanted to yell at her, "*Mo yung lui*, you useless girl!" She stood there like she'd wet herself. She looked weak, this granddaughter of hers. Her blood. How could that be?

Poh Poh waited for the girl's duplicity and the children's greed to disgust her, but the next day, she found herself waiting for their clumsy footsteps to come through the front door. When she showed up with her bag, they cheered.

Every day this went on. Their simple happiness started a small, even glow inside her. She didn't smile or speak, but it was there, a tiny light. During those afternoons, Poh Poh started picking up some English from them. They taught her the name of her favourite chocolate bar: Aero. The word sounded like *arrow*, a straight shooter, the brown boy, Nav, told her. She knew about those.

When they all talked at once, their babble sounded like chickens. She was happy not to understand them and their nonsense. The four of them were of different shades. It had amazed her when she first arrived that June had such a collection of friends. This country was as white as the January landscape until, she realized, you looked more closely. June's best friend, Josie, was another Chinese girl from Hong Kong. Poh Poh wished June could be more like Josie. Josie always cleaned up the wrappers after their afternoon feasts of candy and thanked Poh Poh politely.

Darren was dark brown with hair that looked like a tangle of wire. He had a large laugh and beautiful cheeks. Nav, the brown boy with huge, gentle eyes, was her favourite. Nav had restraint, only accepting whatever Darren broke off his own bar to share, never grabbing, never noisy. She'd never seen a boy with such large eyes, large like a Japanese cartoon character, yet he kept them cast down, and he walked as if hesitating, trailing after the others, hanging on to their edges. She found herself noticing this child in a way she never noticed children. Something about him came to matter to her, made her feel like a cracked-open egg. Vulnerability in others annoyed her, but in this boy, it moved her where few things in her life did. The children were in Grade 8, but his body was still small, contained, not gangly like the rest of them. His face, his grace, they were delicate. He tilted his head like a bird to listen. He gazed at June's heart-shaped earrings and pink socks with the same hunger the others had for the candy.

In him there was a secret of something both pleasurable and shameful. Poh Poh saw this.

◇◇◇◇◇

In late fall, Poh Poh noticed that Nav's hair had gotten longer. He had taken to wearing a blue baseball hat with a bird on it. When he took it off, it left his hair flatter and falling over his ears. He had developed a new gesture to flip it, even though it was still too short for flipping. Its shine was like a new table. She wanted to touch it, but she didn't want her rough fingers to ruin its glassy surface. She thought back to her own hair when she was young, hair that had been known across the city. It fell like a bolt of silk down her back, never tangling even when the wind lifted it and swirled it around. When she was a girl, her mother wouldn't allow her to cut it, telling her that she was lucky to be pretty.

One night in bed, shortly after getting married, her new husband had wrapped a finger around her hair and whispered that it was beautiful. In such a moment, her defences down, she had whispered back the contents of her raw heart: she hated it. She hated her hair. She wished she could shave it close to the scalp the way he did. Chu had been surprised, but he told her she should do what she wanted. She was an adult now and married. If he approved, no one could stop her. That was the moment when she knew she cared for Chu. He accepted her for who she was inside.

He was the one to do it, holding curtains of her hair in his hands as he cut, the strands falling around her. Afterward, he gathered the hair into a box and put it beneath their bed. Like Chu's, her new hair was razor-cut at the sides and a little longer at the top, which she combed over with oil. People laughed and said she and Chu looked like brothers, and while Poh Poh was indifferent to their ridicule, Chu was caught off guard by the ugly attention.

All these years later, Poh Poh still didn't know whether he'd been a naive romantic or just stupid. But he panicked, demanded she grow it back. It was the only time he ever ordered her to do anything. She refused. He stopped talking to her. She frequented the barbershop every two weeks, cutting it back closer and closer to the scalp each time. A wound was growing in her husband, and even though she didn't care anymore what he thought, as a nod of concession, she started wearing wigs. They were ugly, synthetic things. Wasp nests on her head, coarse, like a tight hat of hay. She didn't care if she looked terrible. She amassed a collection—short, long, straight, curly, in all different colours. Her customers at the dried goods store grew used to her strange ways. As long as her dried scallops were good, they kept coming. She knew the wigs embarrassed Chu. She wanted them to embarrass Chu. The small, precious fondness that had glowed in her for him had been doused. If he'd truly cared for her, Poh Poh thought, he would have stood by her.

Their daughter was only eight years old when Chu died. She stopped wearing the wigs, pressed her teeth together and ran their shop alone. She haggled harder with the fishermen, made them lower their prices on salted fish and give her better quality. Everyone knew that she had grown hard, but they trusted her hardness and gave her their money. Gradually, her staff stopped calling her Mrs. Chu and referred to her as *Dailo*—big brother, big boss.

Her wigs became like friends, if she understood anything about friendship. She'd named the wigs after her hero: John, Johnny, Wayne, Spaghetti. Of all her things, she'd been sure to bring these with her from Hong Kong, and there they sat, lined up neatly on their Styrofoam heads on her dresser. She spoke to them from time to time, but mostly, she stroked them like cats.

From the moment Chu had cut off her hair, she had never wanted it again, but only wished she had it now, all that lost hair, in the box where Chu had regretfully laid it to rest. She would have liked to pin the hair to Nav's head, so he could borrow from its former beauty and have something to flip over his shoulder.

Poh Poh began to recognize strains of herself in Nav. It was much more gradual than that, this approaching the mirror, the skimming glances at the reflection until it was understood that the expression in his face was so like her own that she kept hidden.

If he was anything like her, she knew his waters were deep and chill, whereas his friends dallied in warm shallows. His friends wouldn't notice him out so far because they wouldn't even know such secret recesses existed. In the deep, there were weedy silences and places to hide.

Poh Poh often caught him looking furtively in her direction. A hidden recognition passed between them, and they continued this way, stealing peeks at each other. Whenever their eyes met, they both looked quickly away. It didn't seem like it was anything, but it was.

One day that winter, Poh Poh was taking a nap and missed the kids coming in. Not seeing her with her candy, they tramped up to her room to get her. They crept in and instantly began cooing over the wigs. They laughed while trying them on, making funny faces in front of the mirror as Poh Poh sat up in her bed. At first, she was angry, until she saw Nav standing by the door, giggling at the others. Poh Poh got up and took the longest one and walked to the door to give it to him—the one she'd named Ringo after John Wayne's character in *Stagecoach*. He took Ringo and went into the bathroom down the hall and shut the door, unnoticed by the three still posing in front of the mirror. After the kids got their candy and grew bored playing with the wigs, they retreated downstairs to settle in front of the TV, and Nav finally came out. Poh Poh was still sitting on her bed, waiting for him. The wig was much too big on him, and the strands hung all over his face. He looked at her directly for once through the tangle of hair. He pulled it off, gently setting Ringo back on the Styrofoam head and offered her a shy smile before joining the others downstairs.

That day changed their pattern. Often, on frigid afternoons that winter, too cold to play outside, the other kids flopped on the rug in front of the TV while Nav snuck upstairs and visited Poh Poh in her room. They said little, but with hand gestures and her limited English, they managed. She introduced him to the wigs, and in time, he came to greet them by name. "Hello, Rooster!" he'd call to the one she'd named after John Wayne's character in *True Grit*. Or, "How are you doing today, Duke?" But Nav's favourite was Mae West, a curly red bob that Poh Poh used to wear at the store for Chinese New Year. It listed precariously on his little head, but the lurid colour looked surprisingly good on him, and it made his huge eyes glisten as he turned this way and that in her mirror. Poh Poh would put a hand over her mouth to hide her smile.

One day, while Nav was preening in front of the mirror and Poh Poh was on the bed, clucking her approval, June came bounding up the stairs and into Poh Poh's room. The boy's eyes went wide as he quickly whipped Mae West off his head. It flew into the air and landed on the pillow. June took a running jump, landing beside her grandmother on the bed, and quickly donned Johnny Number One, a long grey number that Poh Poh had picked up at the Temple Street night market in Hong Kong on a whim because she'd felt like haggling. June, making pathetic sad faces, looked like a wailing mourner hired for a funeral. Then she picked up Mae West and handed it back to Nav, saying something in rapid English. He put it on slowly, unsure. June gave him a thumbs-up.

Poh Poh thought that maybe June wasn't as selfish as she had thought.

June started following Poh Poh around. She'd sidle up beside her in the kitchen, asking her grandmother to teach her how to cut the greens, how to fry an egg, how to steam a fish. Endless questions. She never shut up. Sometimes Poh Poh answered her, and sometimes she told her to go away. June would laugh, knowing when Poh Poh had reached her limit, and run out before her grandmother could swat her with a dishtowel.

June began to visit Poh Poh in her room at night, and they would eat dry roasted peanuts, cracking them between their teeth and throwing the shells in a bowl while June launched into monologues about a boy named Bruce in her mashed-up language of Cantonese and English. Poh Poh half-listened and never commented, and June didn't seem to notice. Poh Poh wondered if June would be the kind of woman who only lived for love or whether she would smarten up and live for herself. As of now, though, it wasn't looking good.

Mei would walk back and forth in the hall, pretending to get fresh towels or look for a bar of soap. *Don't worry*, Poh Poh wanted to shout out through the closed door. *I am not corrupting your daughter.* Mei told her how happy she was that Poh Poh was spending time with June.

Since the candy stash was being shared among so many, it would often run low, so June started going to buy the sweets with Poh Poh. She taught her grandmother how to walk on the slick sidewalks. "See how the ice hides?" June rubbed the tip of her boot against the snow and revealed the shiny ice beneath. "You think you are stepping on snow, and by the time you realize it's ice, it's too late."

With an arm on June, Poh Poh learned to walk lightly, keeping even weight on both her legs and always brushing the snow with the toe of her boot to see if it was obscuring a patch of ice. June, on the other hand, revelled in the slippery walks and wore down the treads of her boots until they were smooth and perfect for taking a running start and sliding across the sheets of ice.

"Watch this, Poh Poh!" Away she would sail with her arms held wide, smooth as a ship leaving the harbour. Poh Poh was impressed that such elegance could come from such a wild thing.

Poh Poh told June about her store in Hong Kong and all the things she had sold there—the best grade shiitake mushrooms, tiny dried shrimps, flattened scallops, large oysters the size of her palm, and abalone that made soup sweet. Nothing like the crap they sold in the Chinatown downtown. She told her about her regular customers, like the cheap Mrs. Chow with her flashy jewellery and the too-tight cheongsams, who always tried to haggle her down past reason. Even thinking of her made Poh Poh's face twitch. "Remember that, June. Only haggle if you don't think it's worth it. Know the worth! That's the most important thing!"

"But how will I know?"

"First, you have to find out what quality is, June. You

will know when you see it. Then, no one can ever cheat you! You have to know a thing's worth."

One afternoon in the spring when Poh Poh was expecting the children, she heard the slam of the door and June's footsteps as she ran up the stairs. Instead of stopping to see Poh Poh, June dashed into her own bedroom and slammed the door. Poh Poh got up from the bed and went to see her. June was lying on her bed with her shoes still on and her head smashed into the pillow. Poh Poh poked at her back to see if the child was sick. "June-ah. June."

June turned around. Her eyes were red from crying.

"What happened?" Poh Poh asked. The girl was crying hard now, fat tears rolling down her face. Poh Poh repeated the question, this time louder, slower. "What happened, June?"

"Poh Poh," she started. Her voice was hoarse and she gulped for air. "I don't know what happened. Nav came to school with his sister's sunglasses on. They were red and the lenses were shaped like hearts. Some of the kids said he looked like a girl." She stuttered on her words, searching for the Cantonese ones, falling back on the English ones. She paused to take a breath, but Poh Poh felt fury rising in her throat and shook her as if to get a faulty toy to keep working.

"At first, he laughed too, so I laughed. It was funny, and we were just playing, but then more kids came and started calling him a girl. Then they said 'fag.' They said Nav was a fag. They were in a circle and kept saying it. 'Fag. Fag. Fag!'"

June was sobbing now. Poh Poh didn't know this word, but by the way June repeated it, she understood the violence in that short word.

"Then they started kicking him. There were too many of them. Older kids we didn't even know. I didn't know what to do. Darren and Josie yelled at them to go away, but they called them names too. They pushed Darren and Josie out of the way and started punching Nav until he fell down. I saw blood. I don't know whose it was."

A cold sweat broke out over Poh Poh's skin.

"Finally, Nav got up and ran. The kids laughed and stood around a minute, then left. I didn't know what to do."

The sight of her granddaughter weeping on the bed, impotence streaming down her blotchy face, filled her with rage. How did she ever get such a weak grandchild? So stupid and self-absorbed. Poh Poh wanted to hit her, stop the horror that flowed out of her. She raised her hand to June, but then she saw the look in June's eyes as she raised her arms to shield herself. The child had never been hit, but she knew enough to cower.

Poh Poh saw something else too. It was the same confusion that had been in Mei's eyes all those years ago when Poh Poh couldn't hold back her anger and slapped her. June had never had to feel that, and her grandmother could see her young mind working hard to understand. Must one body strike against another to create fire? To what end did the world need to burn?

Poh Poh grabbed June, held her tightly and was surprised to feel her own face wet. Later, Poh Poh asked herself what she had been crying for. For a child battered by other children in the history of a world of beat-up children? Yes, that was what it was. It was enough reason.

The next morning, before the sun rose, Poh Poh softly rapped at June's bedroom door. "Wake up. We have something to do today before school starts." She didn't wait for questions, and June didn't ask any. Poh Poh waited outside while her granddaughter dressed.

They started down the street as the first rays of sun lit the sky, casting the street in an apricot glow. Birds were greeting each other from their hiding places. The world was otherwise still, not yet full of voices and cars. Poh Poh looked around. It was beautiful, peaceful like Mei had said. June took her hand while Poh Poh carried a white plastic bag in her other.

Down the street, they arrived at a tidy brick bungalow. Instead of going up the front walk, June tiptoed through the matted grass to the side of the house. Poh Poh followed. June stopped at the second window and crooked her finger for Poh Poh to come forward and look. There, in his bed beneath the window, was Naveen, cocooned in his blanket.

"Nav, Nav," June whispered, and lightly tapped on the window with her knuckle. She did it again a few more times until he turned and looked up at them.

"It's us, me and Poh Poh. We have something for you."
She smiled.

Poh Poh admired June's smile. It was lovely, very pretty.
It had her heart in it.

Nav crawled out of his bed and came to greet them at the
window. Poh Poh was not prepared for what she saw when
his face turned toward them. The light from the sunrise fell
on him like a veil, revealing the purple bruises around both
of his eyes. His nose was swollen into a bulb. Dried blood
was crusted around his lips. He opened the window with
some difficulty. Poh Poh handed June the bag to give to Nav.
She knew June had already guessed what was in it.

"Here." June pushed the bag over the windowsill.

Nav took the bag and put one hand into it. He smiled,
recognizing the feel of the object with his fingers. He slowly
pulled it out, and Mae West, in all her coppery beauty, lay in
his hand like a promise.

Rain

The year that began with Rainey McPhee deciding whether she would live or die, Rainey's mom moved them to Scarborough, which may or may not have had anything to do with Rainey's decision or its outcome.

It was the middle of October 1981, and seventeen-year-old Rainey was beginning Grade 12 at a new school. Through what turned out to be some sidewalk arrangement between her mother and one of their new neighbours, it was agreed that the neighbour's daughter, June, would show up every morning to walk Rainey to school. Rainey hadn't been informed of this plan, so she thought it was a little weird when a thirteen-year-old Chinese girl appeared at her door at 8:45 a.m. to accompany her that first morning. Fortunately, Rainey was not fazed by much, and June turned out to be all right. She came on time and didn't mind that they walked in silence.

This new school was more or less like the last one. The kids had different faces, but they were the same jocks, cheerleaders, losers and stoners that existed at the other school. Rainey was still a loner, something she couldn't change even if she wanted to. Arriving at school over a month after the fall term had started meant everybody was already settled in their social stations and lunchroom positions. She could tell they were curious about her—the fact that she sported a crewcut certainly set her apart. She also never smiled, didn't like to look anybody in the eye. Walking through the unfamiliar halls, Rainey didn't feel either comfortable or uncomfortable. She was used to the sensation of numbness and didn't even mind it when the kids stared at her.

After a week or so, when Rainey finally asked why she always came knocking, June shrugged and said her parents made her. They wanted Rainey to feel welcome. Rainey wondered if they'd considered that not only was she more than three years older than June, and that they didn't even go to the same school, June's middle school being all the way across the field from her high school. Still, every morning, her giant canvas knapsack strapped across her chest, June dutifully trekked the five doors down, rang the doorbell and mumbled, "Hi, Lorraine. You ready?"

Rainey had a fleeting thought that maybe her mother paid June to come every morning to make sure she went to school. Maybe June was in fact a thirty-year-old private detective or a really short security escort. Rainey knew that with Chinese people, you could never tell how old they were. Sometimes June's best friend, Josie, came with her to Rainey's door. The two of them were like the twins from *The Shining*. They looked identical and sounded identical. Their private conversations sounded like a foreign language, with made-up words, inside jokes and knowing looks passed between them. Rainey was less than impressed on the days she had two private detective escorts to school. Other times, when Josie was off doing one of her many jobs, it was just Rainey and June.

On one of those fall mornings almost chilly enough to wear a ski jacket, as she and June passed the desolate house on Winifred Street, Rainey finally decided to ask June about it. The house wasn't exceptional, the same as most of the houses on the street, but it had no blinds, a shingle was waving in the autumn wind like a loose tooth, and the grass in front was overgrown. It was the only house to stand empty and neglected in a neighbourhood where people had so much pride of ownership, snipping and raking their front lawns within an inch of their lives.

June looked surprised at the question. Rainey rarely said more than a word or two. "It's one of the parent suicide houses, *and* it's haunted—who'd ever want to live in it? Duh!" Then in an instant, June's face turned red. "Um, what I mean is . . . um . . ." She squinted as she glanced sideways at Rainey. Rainey didn't know June at all, but she suspected that June had been told to treat her especially delicately. She kept her face placid, and they walked the rest of the way to school in silence. Parent suicides? She didn't know what June was talking about, but she was intrigued.

At the new school, Rainey didn't talk to anyone, so her second conversation of the day, like a bookend, would come in the evening while her mom hurried around the kitchen, putting together dinner. Between the chopping and stirring, doing her best to be engaged and make eye contact, her mom would ask her questions. There wasn't ever much to tell. Rainey fed her one-word answers to questions about her classes that would at least prove she'd been going.

Her mom filled the gaps with chatter about her new job at the law office, where she was a secretary. She had been a legal secretary up north too. Her mom warbled on like a budgie with exaggerated enthusiasm. "Everybody at work is so *nice*. We all eat lunch together. There's a lunchroom! They even have one of those new microwave ovens, which means I can make hot food! And the way the office is decorated is so *nice*. Burgundy vinyl couches in the reception. Can you imagine? Proper seating like it's a living room! And you know the best part? There is an intercom system, which means I don't have to walk back and forth passing calls and messages. I can stay at my desk and tell them over the phone! Can you believe that? I get so much more work done that way."

Her mom talked and talked as if she didn't know what would happen if she stopped. She knew her mom was trying and, entirely for her sake, Rainey let her continue in her nervous energy. It had been her mom's idea to move. A fresh start, she had said, would be good for them.

Rainey didn't care. There were more people here than in the last place they lived, which was heavy on cows and less so on teenagers. It didn't matter where they were. The blankness inside her had followed her, and she figured it always would no matter where they ended up. Her mother didn't understand it as blankness. She assumed, like the doctor, that it was simply sadness—if sadness could be simple, like a heavy veil that comes on and nudges you into a pit, but eventually, it lifts and you find a way to climb out and get back to normal. A difficult state but a temporary one. She knew her mom was always looking for signs that Rainey had fallen. At the end of every dinner, her mom asked her, as if the whole ritual of chirp-dinner-chirp was merely a preamble for this one moment, "Rainey, have you taken your medication today?"

If Rainey had been someone who had things to rebel against, who needed to test her boundaries to assert her independence and take a stance in the world, she could have gotten away with anything. But she wasn't like that. When Rainey shaved off all her hair, her mother didn't even flinch; she told her it looked darling and followed by cutting her own. She didn't shave it to the scalp like Rainey had, but she did cut her butt-length hair to above her shoulders. Her mother claimed it made her look like Helen Reddy and broke out into the chorus of "I Am Woman."

It wasn't like she was trying to get attention or call for help. Rainey didn't even know why she'd shaved her head. After her father died, she had spotted his old razor in the medicine cabinet one day and thought doing something rash would make her feel something. Most everything of her dad's had been cleared out of the house. The clothes had all gone to charity. Gone were his books, his smell. The razor had somehow escaped her mother's purge.

She was doing it—first cutting the long strands that were not quite to her bum like her mother's but most of the way down her back. Then she rubbed baby oil onto her head and pulled the razor across her scalp. She had felt wonderful. Her heart was beating sure and strong, and she sweated with the effort of the task. It was the most excited she had felt in a long time. But afterward, when her head was clean of hair, and her sweatshirt bore a tangled mess of it, the emptiness returned. She looked in the mirror, her eyes appearing huge in what now seemed like a tiny head. Shadows hung underneath her eyes, the colour of spilled ink on paper. Devoid of hair, she could see the shape of her skull. Rainey was surprised to see how thin she had gotten, the sharp angles of her cheekbones and jaw. Her skin was ghostly pale, and when her eyes trailed down from her face to her neck to her arms, she paused there, noting that her arms were so white, they seemed alien, as if absent of blood, of life. That was when she brought the razor to her wrist. At the time, she'd admired the hue of deep scarlet blood that rose against her too pale skin.

It was so beautiful. She admired it and let the red spread on her canvas of white. For a moment, she felt something like inspiration, like a deep swallow of water after being parched and not even realizing the thirst after bearing it for so long.

The doctor at the hospital kept asking her why—something murky and dark and deep must have happened. She couldn't explain how it felt when she had made the cuts. It wasn't death that she was choosing. Quite the contrary, it had made her feel alive.

The doctor persisted, inquiring about her father's death. It was a place to start, but Rainey was vacant of emotion, like a hotel filled with empty rooms. The doctor asked her about life before her father died, and she thought about how she sounded typical when you looked at the facts. She had been on the verge of starting junior high; she'd gotten her period for the first time; she had friends. And right up to his heart attack, her father had loved her, and she remembered that love, how tangible it had felt, like a morsel of the best cake, the sweetness meeting all the right taste buds in her mouth, lingering long after.

Five years after her father's death, Rainey still felt outside of things, like she was separated from everybody by a pane of glass. Maybe she had felt this way even before her father died, and maybe the feeling just thickened after. She couldn't remember. When she tried to recall the past, it ran like a slow-motion film reel, skipping in places and full of holes. The only time she almost cracked was when her mother had broken down and cried—something Rainey had never seen her do even when her father died of a heart attack—as Rainey lay on the white sheets of her hospital bed, her wrists tightly bandaged. Everything was so bright and blinding, reminding her of her arms, and she struggled to make her eyes stay open. Her mom's sobs filled the brightness, sharpening its intensity. She made a feeble attempt to tell her mother that she didn't want to die, but the words were stuck because she didn't know.

Now her days revolved around a new school, her mother's forced cheer and medication that she never took. She flushed it down the toilet every morning. The pills made it hard to walk, talk, think, as if she were even more dead inside than she already felt. She didn't tell her mother this because she didn't want to break her mother's heart again. If she could go through the motions of living, she hoped it would be enough. Some days, it was. Some days, she wished the glass walls around her would smash into pieces, and she could step away from the splinters and feel whole again. It had been so long since she had felt anything that the years prior felt like someone else's memories.

The day after their discussion about the house, when June came to pick her up, Rainey was ready with her questions. June tilted her head in suspicion at Rainey's sudden need to talk.

"You said something about parent suicides yesterday. Like, plural. When we bought our house, it was a quick sale, so we got to move in after two weeks instead of two months, which the real estate agent said was unusual. Did someone kill himself in there too?"

June nodded quickly, looking as if she was relieved that she could finally tell the truth. "Uh-huh, my softball coach blew his brains out in the basement. Some people say pieces of his brain are still stuck to the walls. Is it true?" June's eyes bugged out wide.

"Oh . . . So that's what's on the walls . . . Hmm. Maybe I'll show you sometime, June."

They'd arrived at the point in the field between their two schools where they always parted. Rainey started to turn away. June put her arm out. "That's not all. There were more—parents who killed themselves in our neighbourhood, I mean. At almost the same time! The houses took some time to sell. Like yours. And that other empty one, the Bevises'."

Rainey turned back to June and considered the kid's face. Could this be true? Rainey's heart thumped, she realized, with excitement.

"I don't know what happened. I still think about it even though no one wants to talk about it anymore." June's voice dropped to a whisper, and Rainey recognized the fear behind June's eyes. She had seen it before. People had been afraid to talk to her after the razor incident. They didn't understand why anyone would choose to die. Because of this fear, Rainey had never tried to explain to anyone the vividness of being close to death, how life paled in comparison.

"Tell me about the other ones."

No longer interested in making the bell, June turned them around and took Rainey back into their neighbourhood on a tour up and down the streets and filled her in on their gruesome history.

"That house, the one I told you was haunted? That was Mrs. Bevis. Hung herself in the bathroom, I heard. No one will buy it because any time someone comes to look at it, the ghost of Mrs. Bevis slams doors and screams. It's true. I heard it from my friend whose dad is a real estate agent. All the agents have given up trying to sell it. It freaks them out to have to go show that place. Mom said maybe her husband cheated on her? Mom said that because once Mrs. Bevis's husband gave her the snake eyes. You know? The snake eyes? Yeah, I don't either. It might be one of Mom's Chinese things . . ."

They walked past a duplex with the garage door open. A teenager about Rainey's age was sitting in the garage on a lawn chair, facing the street. He wasn't doing anything but sitting, smoking, his eyes on them. A radio sat on the ground beside him, tinny sounds of AC/DC coming out. He only had on a lumber jacket even though the sky was white-grey with unshed snow. He had dark hair, wavy more than curly, which hung around his shoulders. It didn't seem like he was interested in making the bell either.

176

June quickened her steps to get past the house, and gave a quick wave to the guy as they passed, and he nodded slowly back. After they had walked a few paces away, June whispered, "That was the second suicide. His mother drank bleach. Foamed from the mouth." June twirled her finger beside her forehead and let her tongue loll out. She pointed out a house with closed curtains as the neighbourhood thief's place. "Watch out for that Mrs. Johnson. She doesn't come out much anymore, but tell your mom to keep her doors locked when you're not home." Rainey realized that her hunch was right, that June had a lot of information under her hat.

The minute school ended that day, Rainey ran home, threw down her bag and went down to the basement. It was colder down there than the rest of the house. She inspected the walls by running her hands across their smooth surfaces. No signs of brain. She sat cross-legged on the carpet in the middle of the room. The carpet was plush and still smelled new. She remembered the real estate agent had made a big deal about the wall-to-wall rug in the hard sell he gave Rainey's mom. Now, knowing there'd been a brain explosion, it made sense. She stared up at holes left by nails and wondered what used to hang there, wishing the walls could talk.

It was macabre, Rainey knew, trying to connect with a space that had been home to a suicide, but she had been curious about death, had felt a kinship with it in a way others didn't. Maybe it began even before her father's death. When she was four and her cat got run over, she didn't feel sadness as much as a feeling of completion, as though life had in some small way come full circle.

When she was seven and her granddad passed, Rainey let herself wonder what death felt like, even desiring to feel it for herself. She had taken her dad's shovel and tried to dig a hole in their backyard vegetable garden, so she could lie in it like her granddad in his coffin. Her mother had found her asleep in a pit, curled in the fetal position among the tomatoes, dirt-smeared and weak from the sun. She did it again, even attempting to bury herself by pulling the soil over her body. She wanted to be enshrouded in complete darkness, until she couldn't see or breathe or feel. Her parents finally got rid of the garden plot and covered it with stone tiles, calling it the new patio.

As she grew older, her thoughts often lingered on thoughts of death. When her father died, she tried to strangle herself with a belt, holding her breath with the hope that she would pass out. Maybe she would be able to see her dad and granddad. To her disappointment, she was never able to hold tight to the belt in the last moments. She hid the red welts on her neck with makeup and scarves.

At night, her dreams took her into other regions, layers of sheer veils lifting to reveal alternate worlds where she believed death resided. In these dreams, she grew weightless until she was airborne, and she glided through magical starlit landscapes. The air in her dreams was always humid and warm. Shadows danced around her as if welcoming her to their realm. She would wake up with a start, believing that she'd been pulled back from death. Each time, she would be left with a lingering memory of the place: the ghostly silver light, the tinkling silence like music, and an ache to stay. Instead of emptiness, Rainey was convinced that death was full: a state of grace. The thought that her granddad and dad felt this comforted her.

She lay on the basement carpet and immediately felt warmth radiating from a place on the carpet to her left. She shuffled over to the spot and was instantly flooded with a feeling of relief. The baseball coach must have been standing right there when he ended it all. She felt a cascade of calm flow over her. Her blood coursed through her body; her skin flushed. It only lasted a few seconds, but she felt more alive than she'd felt in a long time, even more so than when she cut her arms. Alive to Rainey was a kind of humming in her body, a reminder that she was flesh and blood. She had expected to experience death as a black emptiness, but now she realized that the closer she got, the more alive she felt. She found this strange and wondered if this was the irony of death or its black humour. She sat up and wondered if she would feel this same way in the spots where others had ended their lives.

One afternoon some weeks later, right after the first snow-fall, she was turning the corner in the north corridor at school and smacked into Mr. Lumberjack, the guy with the dead mother. She fell right on her ass from the force of the impact. He picked her up as if she were as light as a bird.

"Hey, be careful," he said to her, still holding on to her arm.

She snatched herself out of his hand. "You be careful," she retorted. She felt a rare flash of anger, like a small red spark hopping off her chest. She did not like being embarrassed and rarely felt it.

"You okay?" he asked.

"Yeah." She brushed dust and some bits of spiral notebook paper off her jeans.

"You moved in on my street, right?"

She nodded.

"I'm George," he offered.

"Lorraine." She hugged her backpack.

"Nice to meet you. See you around." He smiled before walking off. He had a nice smile, one that seemed real and not just for the sake of politeness. She didn't usually notice details about people. She watched him disappear down the hall before she turned and continued to class.

After that, Rainey started to look for him. At home, she found that if she stood to the far left of her bedroom window, she could see his house. She was a few doors south on the other side of the street and the angle made it so she couldn't see inside his garage, but she could tell when the garage door was open, a sure sign that George was sitting on his lawn chair with his radio on. At night, there was a truck in the driveway, but it never parked inside, not even in bad weather. When George wasn't there and the pale yellow aluminum door was closed, she would feel disappointed and keep checking until it was open again. It was open most nights even when December came and snow started covering the driveways. When she knew the door was open, she fell asleep more easily. It was the kind of drifting off that reminded her of when she was small and would fall asleep listening to her parents' soft voices and laughter rising from where they would sit and watch TV in the living room.

She wondered if he sat in the garage like she sat in her basement. Maybe he was like her and being close to death also made him feel better. Rainey began looking for George at school, slowing down in the quad to gaze at the rockers hanging out in the "smoking lounge," a small alcove framed by low benches and a pockmarked wall. The boys mostly had long hair and lumber jackets and the girls wore bunny-tail roach clips and fringed leather purses. Rainey studied their easy manner, the girls with their long feathered hair, leaning on each other while they took hits off each other's cigarettes, and the boys eyeing the girls' butts. George was there sometimes, standing with the others in loose circles, all of them stamping their feet to keep warm. They never seemed to notice her.

One morning, she asked June about him.

"George? What do you want to know?" June scrunched up her face.

"I don't know. Tell me about him." Rainey tried to sound casual.

"I don't know. He lives with his dad. They keep to themselves. They're Portuguese. You already know his mom offed herself. That's about it." June paused. "Hey, do you have a crush on him?"

Rainey rolled her eyes. "Never mind, June," she said, but June already had a huge shit-eating grin on her face.

One night, after her mother had gone to bed, Rainey decided she would go see him. It was a Friday, and Rainey was down in the basement, listening to the radio and smoking cigarette after cigarette, stubbing them out in a coffee tin. It was her new thing. The news kept droning on that air pollution was as bad as smoking, so she figured it didn't matter if she added to the pile. Thankfully, her mom didn't let on that she knew about it, even though the house reeked of it.

Rainey had made the basement her special place. Lately though, she'd noticed that each time she returned to the spot where the previous owner died, the once-intense pulsing energy diminished, until it was now only a faint hum in her body. She longed to feel the flood of life inhabit her again, feel that sharp heat fly off her fingertips.

She told herself she was going to George's house for the chance to visit another suicide site and maybe get a hit of that wonder, and that it was incidental that George lived there. She was in her pyjamas and slippers, and before she could change her mind, she wrapped a robe around her tightly and slipped out of the house. The street lamps lit up the light flurry of snow. She didn't feel cold, but she was slipping around on the sidewalk. As she got closer, she heard "Hotel California" coming from his radio. She slowed her steps, ready to turn back. Rainey worried what he might think, that maybe she liked him or something. Or that she was a nutso wandering around in her pyjamas.

Just as she was starting to feel cold and a little ridiculous, and thinking about turning around, he called out to her, "What are you doing? You're gonna freeze!" He jumped out of his chair. It looked like she had scared the shit out of him, and she paused and let herself picture what he must have seen: a pale, skeletal thing wafting silently in the night like a ghost in a plaid flannel robe and soaked slippers.

"Couldn't sleep," she said. She felt stupid standing there in front of him, shivering while snowflakes collected on her robe. A dim lone bulb hanging from a wire from the middle of the ceiling cast the garage in a yellow glow.

"Here, sit." George pulled out the other lawn chair that was leaning against the wall and opened it up beside his. She sat down while he went deeper into the garage and rummaged around before pulling out a blanket. He unfolded it and draped it over her lap. It was red, heavy and smelled like mothballs. Immediately, she felt enfolded in a bright pink warmth that rose through her. She knew she was sitting right on the spot where his mother had died.

"You wanna beer?" She shook her head. He sat back down. "Can't sleep, huh? Yeah, I get that."

Rainey looked at his face. He had a tuque pulled down low over his forehead. He took a swig of beer from his can and continued to gaze into the white-streaked dark.

"So, this is where your mom died?" She knew she shouldn't say anything, but she couldn't help it. He turned his head to face her for what felt like a long time. She held her breath and looked back at him. She couldn't read what he was thinking, but he was studying her carefully.

"Yup. Kinda where you're sitting right now."

She wondered if he said that to shock her. She was careful to register nothing on her face. He smiled, and she breathed again.

"You miss her?"

"Yeah." They unlocked their eyes and turned to watch the snow fall. Fleetwood Mac came on. "Do you like this song?" George asked. He started to sing along.

Even layered over Stevie Nicks, his voice sounded good. With him singing into the darkness, the snow, all of their neighbourhood asleep, it was weird, but it all seemed to fit. The song ended, and Rainey regretted it being over so soon. A Bowie song came on next.

George looked at her and cracked a smile. "You kind of remind me of Ziggy Stardust."

She guessed it was her short buzz cut and blue eye shadow.

"Those cheekbones," he said, nodding. "Man, you have a gorgeous face."

"Oh, shut up." She didn't know how to take that. Was this how boys flirted with girls? She looked down at her hands, willing herself not to blush.

"Yeah. It's all good!" He laughed. He stood up and proceeded to air guitar.

Rainey laughed. A real laugh. She caught herself and wondered if it was because she was sitting on top of George's mother's death, but then realized it wasn't that. Her laughter burbled out of her like a spring.

She began to spend more time with George in the garage. After a while, George left her lawn chair open and ready for when she would join him. She always shifted the chair to be exactly on top of the spot where George's mother died. The flash of pink from the spot would warm her for a few seconds, then subside, but still linger in a soft way inside her body, buzzing quietly. Mostly she and George looked out into the night and listened to music together. George was also not a big talker, which suited Rainey fine. When the nights went from plain cold to icy, George plugged in a space heater.

Rainey's mom was baffled. Why would they insist on sitting in a freezing garage with the doors wide open? Still, she was so relieved that Rainey had made a friend, she didn't push it.

One night, she even intercepted Rainey at the door

with a Tupperware container of cookies and Thermos of hot cocoa. "You two can share," she said.

"Mom, we're not five," Rainey said, trying to squeeze past her, but her mom insisted and made her take everything.

Rainey wondered about the long line strung across the garage. Finally, she asked him about it. George shrugged. "That's where my mom hung the laundry."

"That's a good idea," she said. It was. Dryers were hard on clothes. He nodded. After a while, she felt her face heat up and she blurted out, "I think I tried to kill myself once. That sounds weird, but I'm not sure if I really wanted to or not."

"Oh yeah?" The music had gone crackly and he leaned forward to fiddle with the dial.

She waited a moment. When he didn't say anything, she said, "Don't you want to know about it? You know, considering your mom committed suicide?"

"Nope." George shifted in his chair and twisted the dial again even though the reception sounded fine.

"I would want to know. Hell, I wish I could talk to your mom and ask her what she was thinking. Because I don't even know why or what or anything. Why did I do it?" Rainey shuddered, maybe from the cold, maybe from revealing so much. It was probably the most she had said in a long time, and it didn't even make sense.

186

He sighed. "Lorraine. My mom was fucking crazy. That's why. I don't know how she got that way. It may have had something to do with my fucking crazy dad. All I know is that sometimes, there is no 'why' or 'because.' It's fucked up."

"So, you're okay with it? Like you're over it?" She couldn't stop pressing ahead for something even though she noticed the tension between them.

"What are you, a shrink? No, I'm not okay. I'm not over it. What do you think? She was my mother. Sometimes it was like she was the kid and a pain in the ass on top of that. But do I wish it didn't happen? Of course, I wish she were right here instead of you with your stupid questions."

He wouldn't look at her, and he didn't raise his voice, but she knew he was angry.

"Why do you sit here? Are you trying to stay close to her? Do you feel her here?" Rainey persisted.

"Get out!" George stood up and faced her. "Get out!" He wasn't yelling, but his voice echoed off the empty street.

Rainey stood up quickly, knocking over her lawn chair and spilling the blanket on the ground. She ran home. The radio was playing "I Go Crazy." The irony was not lost on her.

The next day, Rainey sent June off alone, saying she had cramps. After waiting until everyone would've emptied out for the day, she decided to break into the empty house. If George thought she was nuts, she thought she might as well go all the way. June had told her that the neighbour Mrs.

Bevis, who'd lived there, had hanged herself in the upstairs bathroom.

It was easy to get in. Rainey climbed over the fence and slid open a back window. She was small enough to fit through it. The house was cold, but there wasn't anything particularly creepy about it—it was clean and free of cobwebs and other telltale signs of hauntings. The only thing that made it feel spooky was how bare it was. In the kitchen, dusky shadows outlined where the appliances had been. The windows were bare, so Rainey edged along the white walls, hoping no one would see her. She crept through steadily and quietly, as if it were church, her shoes clicking gently on the parquet floors. In each room, she waited for a trace of this dead woman's life to arrive, that familiar warmth that would come, but nothing revealed itself. The house held on to its secrets.

She proceeded upstairs, passing empty bedrooms, and stopped upon arriving at the bathroom. Unlike the rest of the house, which was white throughout, the bathroom on the second floor was papered in powder blue with rows of fluttering silver birds. The tub, the toilet and the basin were also blue. Strangely, there was a striped blue and white shower curtain still hanging from the rod. Why was this left when the house had been stripped of everything else?

She opened the curtain to reveal the matching blue tiles on the wall. Someone had cared enough to make sure this small bathroom matched in every way. Rainey touched the curtain rod gently with her fingertips, feeling small sparks of electricity. This was the place. She sat on the edge of the tub, preparing for the warmth to wash over her. She closed her eyes, her hands pressed against the cold porcelain and imagined the woman stepping off the tub's edge. She began to feel something, but instead of the familiar calm, she was gripped by an immense sadness. Out of the fog of this feeling, images appeared to her, first of a dark-haired woman laughing with a baby in her arms, which soon sharpened into her mother and herself. Then, her father. Her father with his arms open wide but a step away so she couldn't reach him.

Rainey opened her eyes to make it stop and met her own face in the mirror above the sink. She noticed that her eye shadow matched the bathroom decor perfectly. She moved closer to the mirror to get a better look, slipping off the tub and landing on the floor. Splayed on the cold tile beside the toilet, it all suddenly felt absurd. Sneaking into an empty house, finding the place where someone killed herself, so Rainey could feel more alive. She wanted to laugh at how ridiculous it was, but it came out in tears instead.

She moved back to sit on the tub and was chilled by the cold surface. Wiping her eyes, she imagined how this blue had once delighted the former residents. Blue had been her and her father's favourite colour when she was a kid. They were always trying to convince her mother, whose favourite colour was yellow, that blue was the superior hue. Sky and sea trumped sun and flowers. Element pitted against element. Whenever a choice had to be made about colour, she and her dad would yell, "Blue!" Blue skirt, blue icing, blue umbrella. Her mother would throw her hands up in mock surrender while Rainey and her dad would hoot in victory. This joy coupled with its match in sadness. This shade of blue.

She felt sorry for the moment the blue lost its power on the woman who died here. But Rainey then felt grateful that she was able to witness the beauty of it. The blue, like the sky and sea, would always be there, and always be there for her. She let the blue inhabit her and was filled by the bigness of it. She hoped its magic would never abandon her, unlike Mrs. Bevis.

That night, while her mom was standing at the counter, putting together a salad, Rainey snuck up from behind and wrapped her arms tightly around her waist. Her mother paused, her salad tongs mid-air. "I love you, kid," her mom whispered. Rainey nodded against her back and let go gently before going into the dining room to set the table. Rainey smiled when she heard her mom resume tossing the lettuce. That night, she stayed downstairs so they could watch *The Carol Burnett Show* together. They spread out on the couch under one blanket and ate an entire bag of Humpty Dumpty chips.

That year, the winter dragged as if reluctant to leave. It snowed heavily all through March, and Rainey took to joining the neighbours before school in the mornings to shovel the street's driveways and sidewalks. They came to know her. She started doing odd jobs like babysitting Nick and Francesca's baby daughter up the street so they could go on "date nights." The neighbours would wave or nod at her, and she would say hi and smile back, her breath coming out in little puffs. Her dad used to call it "making clouds." These small contacts made her feel like she was becoming familiar to everybody, even herself. She still walked to school with June, with June doing most of the talking. And Rainey had made a couple of friends at school who ate lunch with her in the cafeteria, rocker girls who wore motorcycle jackets, wrote song lyrics in their lined notebooks and hated the cheerleaders. As for George, he never opened his garage door anymore, so she didn't know if he still sat there. Sometimes she passed him in the hall at school, and they both said hello like people who didn't really know each other.

One night at the end of March, the doorbell rang while Rainey was eating a turkey sandwich for dinner in front of *Hawaii Five-O* because her mom was working late. She rose reluctantly, hoping it wasn't a Girl Guide. They were cute and she felt bad turning them away because she didn't like the cookies.

It was George. The sight of him stirred her. He kept his eyes on the mat. "Hey, wanna come sit in the garage and listen to music?" He was wearing his lumber jacket, his hands deep in his jeans pockets. He shrugged like it was no big deal that he was at her door. His hair peeked out from underneath his wine-coloured tuque and grazed his shoulders. She had the urge to reach out and pull the curls so she could watch them spring back.

"Sure," she said. She went to get a coat, her heart beating a little faster.

They walked in silence back to his house and plunked into their usual chairs. She didn't bother to move hers over to the spot. George turned on the radio, and they sat in silence, facing the darkening street. Earth, Wind & Fire's "Reasons" was playing. The air was cold and thick and soon it began to rain, but Rainey didn't feel cold at all. George reached out a hand to feel the drops. The light rain hit the pavement and shot back up, spraying their faces.

"Spring's coming," she said.

"So it is," he answered.

That Time
I Loved You

The summer before we started Grade 9, my parents let me go to Josie's house for a birthday sleepover even without her parents home. I'd launched the campaign about a month earlier, and days of arguing and nagging and negotiating either wore them down or annoyed them to the point where they would do anything to shove me out the door for a night.

"I don't understand why you can't go to the party and come home and sleep in your own bed. What's the difference?" At the last minute, my dad was still determined to make it difficult, but I wasn't going to back down.

"You used to let Josie's sister babysit me here. It's the same thing. Liz can babysit me over at her house!" I was ready with all the counterarguments.

Mom said, "Okay, *sera, sera*." She'd been watching reruns of *The Doris Day Show* again and I didn't try to make sense of it.

Poh Poh shrugged and told him to let me go, and so, with her word like a foot down, they did. But only because Josie was Chinese and understood which things were right and wrong.

Josie's parents were away the last week of July, and she and her siblings were taking advantage of their freedom and throwing a party. Josie's birthday was a convenient coincidence. Sleeping over meant no curfew, which further meant that I could spend all night at a party and work to achieve the goals I had been holding on to for a very long time: (1) attend my first dance party and (2) (maybe?) win Bruce back.

On the night before the party, Josie and I painted our nails in her bedroom.

"Josie, what do you think we'll be like in ten years?"

Josie's face was scrunched in concentration as she applied shell-pink polish to her index finger. She was a terrible manicurist and always messed up her right hand when she used it to paint her left. I took the brush from her and held her spread fingers in mine.

"I don't know, June. I don't have a crystal ball. Anything can happen."

"We'll always be friends, right?" I didn't like the whininess that was sneaking into my voice, but I persisted. I had been feeling her drift away recently.

"Sure, June . . ."

I nodded, turning back to her fingers. I wasn't convinced that she felt sure. "You're stuck with me. We'll even live on the same street after we're married. Our kids will be best friends too. We're going to be really happy."

"June, you think too much . . . Stop your Jesus talk. Can you put a second coat on for me?"

People were always saying that I thought too much and talked even more. My mom, dad, Josie, Poh Poh, Nav. They all told me so. Was it a crime to think too much? Wasn't thinking supposed to be a *good* thing? Sometimes Josie accused me of doing "Jesus talk." That was her way of saying I was too deep, too intense. I always had too many questions or too many answers. It didn't matter that we weren't religious, that I'd never said a word about God or Jesus or any of that stuff and Josie was the one who went to church. She said that when I got all serious, I reminded her of the priests and their boring speeches about life.

Josie and my parents were lucky that I didn't share half the stuff that I thought about. For instance, I had been thinking about the suicides again. No one wanted to talk about it anymore, like it never happened, but I thought about it more and more. I wondered about what happened to them to make them want to die. I couldn't imagine it. I had bad days, and I knew my parents and Poh Poh did too, but how bad could things get for people to not even want to find out what would happen next? Like, maybe the problems they felt were so hopeless would actually be solved. Or that something so completely good would happen and push away all the bad. It could happen. I thought so. You had to stick around. Were the parents who killed themselves not the stick-around types?

"Tell me who's coming to the party again," I said, steering us to safer ground.

I was excited because a bunch of older kids from downtown were planning to come. It was happening more often that after school, instead of playing on the street with us, the older kids from our group were going downtown to hang out with some Chinatown kids they'd met at the community centre when the Shadow Dragons' volleyball team played. The Dragons, apparently, were the finest of the Chinatown boys. According to Josie, who tagged along with her brother, they were tall, athletic and very cute. She had a crush on one of them, a boy they called Little John. The "Little," she explained, came from the fact that he was a few inches shorter than Big John. She even went out for noodles after the game with them a few times.

My dad thought Chinatown was a rat's nest, and we never went. They didn't even speak our kind of Chinese, so he doubted their noodles were anything to write home about. My mom made the trip to Chinatown every other week to buy gossip magazines and dried shiitake mushrooms for Poh Poh. Even she said she hurried home because downtown was filthy.

My dad said he didn't immigrate to this country only to have me hang out with a bunch of poor Toishan kids from the old country, whose parents worked in garment factories. We were from Hong Kong and not the mainland. We were a British colony like how Canada first got started. This supposedly made us better people. Needless to say, I was never allowed to go. For me, Chinatown remained a dream, the wonderland that was a long bus, subway and streetcar trip away. It was the land of good-looking boys and steaming plates of chow mein with shrimp.

When my friends went to Chinatown on the weekends, I hung out with Nav and Darren. Even though Darren's mother had transferred him to the Catholic school after what happened with Mr. Wilson, Nav and I still saw Darren every day after school. Mr. Wilson got fired after hitting him. Darren never spoke about what happened that day, but he said he liked his new school. He said he was getting good grades now because the rest of the Catholic kids weren't that smart.

I would always remember the day Mr. Wilson punched Darren after accusing him of cheating—that punch and how Darren fell down and got up again, staring at Mr. Wilson as if daring him to do it again. It was hard to think of Mr. Wilson as a bad person because on most days, he seemed like a good guy. He told us stories and was strict, but my dad believed Mr. Wilson wanted his students to be the best they could be.

Darren had been telling us for weeks that Mr. Wilson was out to get him, and the only reason he could come up with was that Darren was Black. "Do you believe me, June?" Darren had asked me. "Yes, I do," I had said, but honestly, I still wasn't sure. It wasn't until the moment when Mr. Wilson punched him that I knew. I promised myself that I would never doubt again that people could be that ugly and mean. It wasn't something you could explain away.

I should have done something that day to help Darren. I had been frozen in my seat from shock, and it never occurred to me that I could do anything to make it stop. It was Nav, the one you'd least expect, who got up and stood between Darren and Mr. Wilson and said, "Enough." That did something to Mr. Wilson, and he left the room. Nav was the brave one even though I had always assumed he needed us to take care of him. It ended up that I was the chickenshit.

We never saw Mr. Wilson again. Still, Darren's mother took him out of our school and transferred him. I wished Darren had stayed, because next time, I would be ready. I felt the same way about Nav getting beat up for being too much like a girl. That Darren stood up to Larry Lems as Nav did to Mr. Wilson made me vow to myself that I would try to have as much guts.

Sometimes Nav, Darren and I went with Poh Poh to the Red Grill at the mall and ate hot chicken sandwiches with gravy. Darren and Nav looked forward to these Saturdays, and I know Poh Poh got a kick out of them too. She had discovered french fries and insisted I tell the server to only give her the "crispy ones," which were the burnt, brown ones. It was embarrassing to ask the acne-faced kid with the metal tongs to select fries for us like picking prize peaches, but Poh Poh got so much glee from those potatoes.

Still, even though our outings were fun, I couldn't help but sulk. I missed my other friends and wanted to meet the famous Shadow Dragons. My parents were awful people. I was ready to go downtown. I was old enough. Why couldn't they see that?

Josie's party was turning out to be an exciting prospect because not only did it mean everybody would be together again, but the Chinatown kids were also coming. Josie was hoping Little John would make an appearance.

Josie and I worked on goal number one by asking her sister, Liz, to teach us how to dance. She said we should start out with the basic steps. It was easy, Liz assured us as we put on our leotards and went into the basement with its freezing concrete floor. "Listen to the beat and step in time to it. Step to the right, step to the left. Add a bit of a bounce. *Ta da*." She left to talk on the phone, and Josie and I practised it a thousand times to Gary Numan's "Cars." After Liz was satisfied with our efforts, she taught us some of Michael Jackson's moves to "Rock with You." I could certainly feel the heat, but as much as we practised, I never could ride the boogie.

Josie did much better and was even coordinated enough to snap her fingers and swing her arms.

Goal two was harder. It had been two years since Bruce and I went around, but I was still hung up on him. I was also in love with John Travolta, but other than that, no one compared to Bruce in my eyes. I felt like a loser for still liking him for what felt like forever. I wondered if I still had a chance. I had started using eyeliner, and although I probably wasn't beautiful, I could pass for pretty. I was still short and skinny and as flat as an ironing board, but Bruce had once told me that I had a nice smile, so I practised new ones in the mirror. So far, my favourites were a lopsided one, one that made my dimples go deep, and a barely-there one too.

I was going to wear the Hawaiian shirt that I had begged my mom to buy for me at Woolco, a white short-sleeved number splashed with large blooms of red hyacinth and purple orchids, along with my yellow Roadrunner jeans. Everybody was wearing Roadrunner jeans, with their signature six chevrons on the back pockets.

Every day, it seemed, Josie droned on and on about Little John and how high he could jump to spike the ball onto the opposing court. I'd let her babble and my mind would drift toward my favourite daydream of my reunion with Bruce. I cringed when I thought about how shy I had been with him and swore that he would see a new June at the party: a teenage babe who would know how to act and what to say. I would be so cool that he would regret ever having given me up. I fantasized about how he'd ask me to slow dance in Josie's basement. As the first chords of Peaches & Herb's "Reunited" played, he would approach me as I stood talking to the cutest Shadow Dragon boy at the party. Bruce, with his hand extended, would ask in his man/boy voice if I wanted to dance. I would slowly turn to gaze at him as if boys asked me to dance all the time. I would hesitate, look back at the Shadow Dragon and regretfully excuse myself before taking Bruce's hand and walking with him to the middle of the room. He would pull me to him, and it would be like we had never parted.

I never shared this with Josie. Even I knew it was way too corny.

On the night of the party, my mom took a Q-tip and covered my eyelids with a baby-blue glittery powder. She took a big brush and drew two big pink lines on my cheeks. When she was finished, she stood back to assess her handiwork. "A face only a mother can love!"

"What do you mean, Mom? I'm ugly?" I asked.

"Huh? Oh no. You look okay," she said as she closed all the lids on her makeup. "So, Josie's sister and brother are going to be there the whole time, right?" she asked.

"Yes. I told you already. They will be there the whole time."

"No alcohol, right?"

"Of course not!" I rolled my eyes.

Poh Poh passed by and when she saw me sitting on the bathroom counter, her eyes widened before she walked away muttering something I couldn't hear. I turned to look in the mirror. I looked different, older. Maybe even almost fifteen? The two additional years satisfied me.

I went over to Josie's house before anybody else arrived. When I got there, I was surprised by Josie's outfit. She was all in black. Black Roadrunners and a black tube top with silver sequins. I had never seen these clothes before. She did a twirl for me in the hallway when I entered.

"Nice, eh? Liz took me shopping today and bought this for me with her babysitting money."

"Yeah. Really nice!" She did look nice, but suddenly I felt like a kid in my Hawaiian shirt.

I helped her and Liz set out all the chips and peanuts. They had made punch and used their mother's crystal bowl. It weighed a ton and was cut with a pattern of winding vines and grapes. Liz had used a special recipe of cocktail fruit concentrate and ginger ale. At the last minute, she put away the ten little matching cups and set a stack of Styrofoam ones out instead.

Nav and Darren came first, at 8:00 p.m. sharp. Darren wore a tie with a denim collared shirt. Nav had wet-combed his hair so hard, the rake marks were still visible on his head, while the rest hung in damp ringlets. He was letting his hair grow now despite his parents' complaints. It was at his shoulders. It suited him, and Poh Poh gave him a new nick-name, *Lang Lui*—"Pretty Girl."

The whole gang from the street followed in quick suc-cession and filed into the basement, following the beat of the music, but no Bruce. I started to worry that he might not show. Tim took over the DJ duties and blasted the cas-sette player to full volume. I decided not to give my whole night over to worry and joined the group. Everybody was dancing to the music. The room was dark except for the small direct light from the desk lamp they'd put over the player and stacks of cassette tapes: Kool & the Gang, Donna Summer, the Bee Gees—all our favourites. Even Nav was dancing, making some kind of jerky move that involved kicking his legs from side to side. I felt like I'd gotten the hang of Liz's tutorial and was starting to enjoy myself with my side-to-side funk move. With all of us there dancing, it didn't seem like Josie's basement anymore—the place with a clunky dryer and where we'd practised skateboarding on the uneven concrete floors as the sun peeped in through the slot of window near the ceiling. Tonight, our music and dancing had transformed the room into the dance studio in *Saturday Night Fever*.

A loud cheer came from upstairs, and Josie bolted from the dance floor and tore upstairs. I heard her squeal. I darted up after her. A small group of Chinese guys I'd never seen before were standing in the hallway. From Josie's and the other girls' reactions, I guessed they were the Chinatown boys. Some of them wore red T-shirts with black dragons printed on the front, marking which ones were the famous Shadow Dragons. They looked like normal boys, nothing like the brown muscled men from my dad's kung fu movies I'd been picturing, but they were cute. One of them looked over at me and didn't stop. I pretended to pick lint off my right thigh, a little disappointed that he wasn't wearing a red shirt. Josie grabbed my arm and pulled me into their circle. She introduced me as her best friend to each of them in quick succession: Frank, Chung, Gord, Jimmy, Harry, Victor, Big and Little John. I gave a little wave. The one, Jimmy, still hadn't broken his stare, and I worried that the blue glitter on my lids must have sweated a line straight down to my chin. Jimmy wasn't a boy, not in the way that Nav and Darren were. And not like Bruce, who seemed trapped between boy and man and still had so much of his childish prettiness with his full lips and high cheekbones. Jimmy looked like a man. He was tall and solid. There wasn't any softness about him. I felt like a bug trapped under a glass, the way he looked at me.

"Is this a party or what?" said the one named Frank as he pulled out a bottle of clear liquid from his knapsack. I was shocked, but Josie smiled this weird plastic smile like Barbie and didn't try to stop him. The rest of the boys cheered. Frank proceeded to pour the bottle into the punch.

Out of the corner of my eye, I saw Bruce in the living room, talking to Tim. He was dressed completely in white:

a white short-sleeved T-shirt and white painter pants. My heart did that strange thing it did whenever I saw him, like it turned upside down, like it didn't quite fit. He and Tim turned at the noise and greeted the Dragons. They all slapped each other on the back and shook hands like real men. Bruce glanced over at me and smiled. I smiled back but still wondered if I had a blue stripe down my face. I hoped to God not. Just as quickly, Bruce turned away and continued his conversation with Tim.

Liz passed around Styrofoam cups of the alcohol-spiked punch. I said I didn't want any when Tim handed one to me. I glanced at Josie. She had taken a cup too, so I grabbed a cup before Tim could walk away.

"Happy birthday, Josie! Cheers!" Frank raised his cup, and we all followed. The living room had gotten crowded since everyone from the basement had come up. We all raised our cups and drank. I was so thirsty, I finished mine in one gulp. It tasted like cough syrup. I felt it travel down a path to my stomach like a line of fire. Jimmy moved over to me and handed me another drink. I tossed it into my mouth again like it was Kool-Aid, trying not to grimace.

"Are you okay? You didn't have to drink it all at once, you know." He seemed nice, but I didn't want to be treated like a child. I nodded like I knew what I was doing, and he scooped up some punch and gave me another. Then we went downstairs to the basement.

Everything began to appear in snatches of colour and

motion. I had never drunk alcohol before and was surprised at how great I felt. The basement was crowded with people moving as if in one big mass to the beat. My body felt loose and limpid like dancing and I were meant to be.

A slow song by A Taste of Honey started to play. It was about geisha girls in Japan or something. Jimmy was beside me in a second. He took my hand gently, pulled me to the centre of the floor and lifted my arms to his shoulders before wrapping his around my waist. I wondered if Bruce saw, but all around me, everyone looked like dark shadows. I hoped Bruce's white clothes would shine, providing a light for me, but Jimmy hugged me close to him, and I couldn't see anymore. A tiny throb began in my head, so I rested it on his shoulder, hoping he didn't mind. I felt dizzy and wanted to go home to my bed.

It went like that for what could have been two hours or two minutes. There were fast songs, then slow songs. Jimmy was there for all of it. At one point, he asked if I was hot. I touched my forehead and it was wet with sweat. He took my hand and led me upstairs. A few bodies were draped over the couch and floor; a few people were eating cake in the living room. Bruce was sitting in the middle of the loveseat. When he saw me, he scowled and turned back to whomever he was talking to. I wondered what his problem was; he'd ignored me. Maybe now that I was holding hands with another boy, he was jealous. Everything felt heavy, even my thoughts, like we were underwater.

He led me to the backyard. It didn't feel any better out-side. The night was thick with humidity.

"Your face is all blue," Jimmy said, half laughing, half curious. I reached my hand up to wipe it. Maybe that's why Bruce looked at me like that. "Here, let me. It's okay. It's cute. You're cute." Jimmy took a corner of his T-shirt and brushed it against my face.

Then he kissed me. It was very gentle, a slight touching of his lips to mine. It felt very different from Bruce's kiss. No teeth were involved, just softness like I had always imagined. I closed my eyes. When he moved his face away, I opened my eyes and looked up at him. Jimmy's eyes were glowing from the half-light coming from the living room window. My father once said that it was never completely dark in the suburbs. Light was always escaping and spilling everywhere.

"You're so pretty, June."

"Thank you."

He pulled me closer to him, but I moved my head to the left so that his lips landed on my cheek. He was a stranger.

"Let's go back inside."

"I like you, June." He gripped my arm.

I nodded. He tried to kiss me again, his hold on my arm tighter this time, too tight to be comfortable. Again I turned my head. I was about to explain, when suddenly he smirked. "You're a tease, aren't you? Fuck this." He pushed me away and stormed off back to the side door and inside. It wasn't even that hard of a push, but I lost my balance and fell on the grass anyway. The screen door slammed against the frame.

I stayed outside on the grass by myself for a while longer, listening to the crickets. Jimmy's anger rolled off of me. I was too numb to feel anything but tired. My brain felt like it was moving through mud. Small lights from other windows interrupted the darkness. They drifted from houses, reaching across the yards, searching for dark corners. The yellow splashes and lines of light looked like they were dancing to the funk music thumping out of the basement. I rubbed my eyes to make sure I knew what I was seeing. The earth was tilting. I stood and, steadying myself against the jagged bricks of the wall, went back inside through the side door. I wanted to see a familiar face. I needed my friends. I wanted to shed my body, the stupid makeup, this party, and have all of us together being normal. I looked for Nav, Darren and Josie, but they weren't upstairs.

People were still lounging around in the living room, and the punch bowl was empty. I made my way slowly down the stairs to the basement, careful to keep the ground from slipping under me. By the time I reached the bottom, I felt the need to barf. The laundry room was straight in front of me, and I pushed the door open and darted in. I didn't know where the light bulb was and started to feel around for the sink. Then movements coming from directly in front of me startled me. I felt the pull chain for the bulb brush against my cheek, and I reached for it. As the light clicked on, it

208

caught the sequins on Josie's top, making her look like a disco ball. Behind her, leaning on the washer, I could make out someone in white. Painter pants. Bruce. They were hugging or something. Kissing. His hand was under her tube top. They both turned and saw me, and my eyes felt like they were blinking so slowly.

"June. It's you." Josie didn't sound surprised to see me. She fixed me with a stare that said this was somehow my fault. Bruce didn't look at me at all, his face turned toward the wall while he retrieved his hand from her top. The bulb swung back and forth on its cord. The light cast them in and out of shadow, still like statues, pressed together, her eyes glued to mine.

Suddenly, I was not drunk anymore. I felt like I had been dunked into an ice water bath and someone was holding my head down. I turned and bolted up the stairs, pushing people out of my way to the door. I kept running outside as I raced up my driveway and to my front door. I paused at the door, breathing hard, and opened and shut it softly, not wanting to be heard. I leaned against it on the inside and waited to feel better.

I didn't know how long I stood there, but when I finally climbed the stairs, I could still feel the imprint of the doorknob on my back. As I walked down the hallway, the slant of light from under Poh Poh's door widened and she peered out. "June, is that you? Are you okay?"

"Yes, Poh Poh. I didn't feel like sleeping over. Go back to bed."

The light disappeared as her door closed, but I could still see a thin, straight line as it crept out from the threshold. I used that light to guide me to my room next door to hers. I didn't bother to change. In the dark, I climbed onto my bed and curled into a ball. My body felt like lead, and my head pounded. I wished I could wake up my mom, but I knew she would freak out when she sniffed the alcohol on me.

I couldn't think about Josie or Bruce right then. I tucked them away for tomorrow, for when I would be able to tell if this night was a dream. Right now, my head was still foggy. I got up and went to my window and felt the night air on my face. It felt stuffy inside me, like I didn't have enough air, so I tried to breathe deeply. From there, I could see the spread of Winifred Street. Everything was quiet except for the low buzz of electricity and the faint music drifting from Josie's house. Even from my window, I could tell it was a slow song. "Endless Love."

The light from the street lamps fell like pools on the black road. Even though I couldn't see the details in the dark, I knew the street like my own face. I knew the curve of the road from my house before it straightened toward Nav's. I knew my favourite part of the curb to sit on to watch Bruce pop wheelies on his bike. I knew the patterns in the wood grain of my front door. I knew the numbers of each of the suicide houses.

When the suicides first happened, my mom had said, "There's more than meets the eye." She had said it as an explanation, but I hadn't given it much thought at the time. I looked down at the dark street and knew now that there were things that lurked on the other side of doors, behind the friendly faces, underneath the polite chatter across the fences. Although I had tried to pay attention to everything, what I thought I knew so well was probably not what it seemed. I thought of Josie's eyes in the basement and knew that she must have secrets too.

The questions that I had had two years ago about the suicides were different from the ones I had now. Two years ago, I had only thought about *how* they did it and didn't think much about *why*. Now it was all I could think about. Maybe one day I would understand. But today, I didn't understand anything—why Josie would hurt me, why Bruce would never be mine, why the parents killed themselves.

I stared out into the night and thought about the one thing that my mom had always said that made more sense to me than anything else: home was where the heart was. Everything that mattered to me—my parents, Poh Poh, Josie, Nav, Darren, school—was here. But what happened when you expected home to be your heart and it wasn't? What then?

I had assumed I would always want to live here, but now I knew that was childish. This neighbourhood wasn't every-thing. It wasn't anything at all, a grid of streets that crossed each other, a bunch of people thrown together. There were other places in the world, and I knew I would go. This place here, it was already leaving me, and maybe this was what it felt like to have your heart break.

Once, I asked Poh Poh if she wanted to return to Hong Kong, and she said that once you left a place, you could never go back and expect it to feel like home. "Places change," she said, "and so do people. Memories sometimes lie."

I listened to the buzz of the street lamps. I thought about those lights and how they had always been my signal. They always told me when to go home. I used to hate the street lights, wishing that the purple and orange glow at sunset would stretch endlessly, so I could remain outside with my friends forever. I wanted to hold on to this picture. This memory would not lie, as my grandmother had warned. A long, long time from now, I would remember the row of lights flickering on as night slowly fell to the street, and all of them waving back at me like shadows as I turned away.

Acknowledgements

As I was writing this book, the characters would follow me around. They rode with me on streetcars, stood in line beside me at coffee shops and accompanied me on dog walks. Some of them spoke to me with urgency, commanding me to put pen to paper and write in fast and furious sessions. Some spoke haltingly. The long silences interrupted by short utterances tested my patience. They made me laugh, and often, they tore me up. I grew to care for these characters deeply, and perhaps it's a strange thing to say, but sometimes, I was just their typist. Writing is a deep magic, and I am grateful that sometimes this magic touches me.

I am immensely thankful to my agent, Denise Bukowski, and my editor, Jennifer Lambert. They recognized a spark in this book when I was still not sure. Working with them has been a privilege.

Thanks to the Ontario Arts Council Writers Reserve program and especially to Diaspora Dialogues and Inanna Publications for their support.

I am indebted to my writing mentor and friend Jenna Kalinsky. It was serendipitous for me to wander into her creative writing class and find my way. Jenna has always been supportive, firm and passionate in her guidance. Her commitment to the craft has inspired me to be a better writer.

My early readers, Lynn Caldwell, Stephanie Dayes, Karen B.K. Chan, Sarah Couture-McPhail, Andrea Fatona and Estelle Anderson offered feedback and nourishment for my mind, body and soul. I am a lucky woman to have the friends and community that I do. There are too many to name here. You know who you are, and if you are not mentioned by name, let's say I owe you a drink . . .

I am eternally grateful for the people who I grew up with in a little pocket of Scarborough, Ontario. My childhood memories of the Tes, the Angs, the Laos and the other kids on my block shaped my imagination from which this book emerged. My thanks especially to Hayley Lao, my first and longest BFF, who taught me how to chop onions, talk to boys and catch fly balls. She possesses the same indomitable spirit today as the first day I met her when we were nine.

Much love to my mom, dad, my aunts, uncles and cousins for being proud to have a writer in the family. I am especially elated to have my brother, Cecil Leung, in my life. My Poh Poh and Gung Gung continue to be my driving force long after they have departed from this world. Thanks also to the Paynes and Archdekins, who provided unwavering support through many years.

To Andrew Archdekin, you are, as always, my family. Your presence in my life is a gift. Thank you for continuing to believe in me.

To my kiddo, my Bean, the heart of my heart, Fenn Archdekin-Leung: you ask me every night to tell you a story. Here's more for you. I hope we keep telling stories to each other forever.

Lastly, while this book refers to suicide, I hope it's also a testament to the resilience we share when faced with the often-difficult work of living. If you are meeting these stories and characters at a heavy moment in your life, I wish you love and solace.